"YOU'RE ASKING ME TO HELP?"

"It's unusual," he said, "but look, you want your boy back, and there's no way in hell I can just hand him over to you. Not now, not the way it looks now. The way I see it, the only way he's going to walk is if someone else did it and we can prove it. Now, you've worked a hell of a lot more killings than I have. But are you sure you're up to working this one?"

"I'm up to it," I said.

"And if you help work it and find out he did do it, then what are you going to do?"

"It won't happen," I said, "because he didn't do it."

———————————— ★ ————————————

"A believable sleuth in a superior series."
—*Booklist*

"Deb's exploits make a heady reading adventure."
—*Publishers Weekly*

"Martin's fiction smacks of reality."
—*The Houston Post*

Also available from Worldwide Mystery by
LEE MARTIN

MURDER AT THE BLUE OWL
DEATH WARMED OVER

Forthcoming from Worldwide Mystery by
LEE MARTIN

DEFICIT ENDING
THE MENSA MURDERS

HAL'S OWN MURDER CASE

LEE MARTIN

WORLDWIDE®

TORONTO • NEW YORK • LONDON
AMSTERDAM • PARIS • SYDNEY • HAMBURG
STOCKHOLM • ATHENS • TOKYO • MILAN
MADRID • WARSAW • BUDAPEST • AUCKLAND

HAL'S OWN MURDER CASE

A Worldwide Mystery/January 1992

First published by St. Martin's Press Incorporated.

ISBN 0-373-26087-3

This book is dedicated to my son Patrick Richard Paul Webb, who has at various times been Paul, Pat, Patrick, and, at last word, Rick. Hal has always been based on Paul—much to Paul's delight—but real sons age faster than fictional ones, and Paul has had many adventures since Hal's worst crime was playing with a Pacman watch in the living room and teasing his sisters. I thought it was time for Hal to have an adventure of his own.

PROLOGUE

THERE ARE SMALL towns in which nothing ever happens. Most small towns fall more or less into that category. And then there are small towns in which everything always happens. Las Vegas, New Mexico, falls into that second category.

I would like to express my appreciation to the charming people of the beautiful state of New Mexico for their courtesy on our recent fact-finding tour to do research for this novel. Special thanks are due to Las Vegas Chief of Police Donato Frank Sena (on whom Salazar definitely is not based), for his helpful attention to a total stranger who barged into his office and began asking questions.

As always, I want to emphasize that the Fort Worth, the Texas, the Los Alamos, the Las Vegas, the New Mexico, and all the people and places in this novel are not quite the real places of those names. All the people, and most of the places, in this novel are completely fictitious.

Dear Mom,
    We have been ~~studing~~ studying atomic en-

ergy in school and Lorie and I thought it would
be fun to go and see Los Alamos during spring
break. You were to busy with Dad and the baby
and everything so we didn't want to ask you and
Lorie's mom was pretty busy to. So we are going to just go there and come right back. We met
this guy at this truck stop, you know the one you
turn at when you are going to the elks, and he
said he'd take us and he said we wouldn't have
any trouble finding a ride back.

Don't worry about us we will be alright and
we will be back by the time spring break is over.

Love,
Hal

PS we left a note for Lorie's mom to.

ONE

I AM GOING TO kill Hal.

Absolutely, positively, without the least possible shadow of a doubt, I am going to kill Hal, I told myself as I reread his note for at least the fourteenth time.

I was going to murder my sixteen-year-old son and pin his hide to the garage door to dry.

Only first, of course, I was going to have to find him.

I suddenly became aware of the telephone. Not sure how long it had been ringing, I hurried to answer it. It wouldn't, of course, be Hal. It would be my husband, Harry, who was laid up in the hospital following an accident with a new prototype helicopter he was test piloting. Or it would be my mother, inquiring about how Harry was doing, and was I sure I didn't need her to come and help me, with my baby due so soon. Or it would be Lorie's mother—Officer Donna Hankins—calling to ask me whether I had found my note yet and what we were going to do about it.

But then on the other hand maybe it *would* be Hal, somewhere the other side of Weatherford, wanting me to come get him and bring him home. Which I would do because he had Lorie with him; otherwise I might be highly tempted to tell him he got there on his own, he could get back on his own.

No, I wouldn't really do that. I'd go get him. Of course I'd go get him.

Only I didn't have the option. I had been right the first time. It wasn't Hal on the phone. It was Donna, somewhat more hysterical than you'd expect a cop to be. But then she's somewhat younger than I am and she hasn't been a cop long. Like me, she's been a mother longer than she's been a cop, but even in that sphere her experience is eight years and two teenagers less than mine. Hal is my third child, and I am more or less used to the insanities one's offspring can create.

There is an old saying—Yiddish, I believe—to the effect that small children disturb your sleep, and large children disturb your life. Well into coping with my third teenager, I would certainly be inclined to agree with that assessment.

It isn't that Lorie is Donna's youngest child, or her oldest. Lorie—who was Laura until she hit the earliest of those ages at which all teenagers want to change their names—is Donna's only child. Which twists Donna's sensibilities even more.

Short of hysteria, Donna's main question seemed to be, What are we going to do about it?

I considered that a pretty good question. I wished that I could think up a pretty good reply to it.

I could not. I told her I'd come over to her house to discuss the matter, and I hung up. Fast.

What her note and my note seemed to add up to was, My son Hal, sixteen, and her daughter Lorie, fifteen, had taken off from Fort Worth, Texas, to hitchhike to Los Alamos, New Mexico, and back—in a week. They had, apparently, left in an eighteen-wheeler they had somehow managed to acquire at a truck stop otherwise notorious for having the largest number of prostitutes in the entire Tarrant County area. How Hal and Lorie had gotten to the truck stop neither of us knew yet; Hal, unlike Lorie, did have a driver's license, but neither Donna nor I was missing a vehicle.

What could we do? Well, we could put them on NCIC, the big national computer that links wants and records for the entire United States. If we did that—if somebody happened to spot them and get curious and run them on NCIC—we'd then know where they were.

I didn't need to tell Donna how unlikely that was.

You run people on NCIC because they are look-ing—or acting—suspicious in some way. If Lorie were traveling cross-country alone somebody might spot her as a potential runaway and get curious. But she wasn't alone; she was with Hal; and nobody was going to spot Hal as a runaway.

Hal—the last time we measured him, which was about two weeks ago when we had to buy him new school jeans for the sixth time this school year—is now six foot five. The doctor tells us, encouragingly he seems to think, that he doubts Hal will put on more than another inch or two. Or three or four.

Hal is adopted. He is half-Korean. Koreans tend to be short people. But the other half, the non-Korean half, must be very, very tall.

All this meant that not even the most cautious po-lice officer, seeing Hal standing on the side of the road hitchhiking, was going to suspect him of being a runaway. Most of the time somebody six foot five is quite old enough to be looking after himself. That, in turn, meant that nobody was going to check on Lorie either, because Hal and Lorie would be quite obviously together.

It would be possible, theoretically, to get on the CB radio and start looking for them that way. Al-most all truckers have CB radios; they live on chan-nel 19.

Harry has a CB radio. I could use it—unlike his ham radio, it doesn't require any kind of license, and all you have to do is turn a couple of switches and press the button on the microphone. Even I know how to do that. I could get on it and ask all the truckers to look for a pair of hitchhikers, descriptions as follows.

Except that a CB radio will carry only so far, and these two were probably well out of its range. Oh, sure, you can ask truckers to relay—and they will. If Hal and Lorie were ten-year-olds, that very efficient truckers' network would have every truck driver in the contiguous United States looking for them in a couple of hours. But truckers tend to be more or less free spirited. Given the circumstances, they would probably figure that Hal and Lorie are old enough to be doing whatever they want to and Donna and I are just interfering busy bodies.

So this time the radio wouldn't do any good.

It would be pleasant to be able to convince myself the truckers' assumption was correct. A six-foot-five sixteen-year-old high school sophomore ought to be able to look after himself and someone else, especially if he is of normal intelligence and has been raised by two basically responsible parents, and on top of that has been, for a couple of years and quite voluntarily, attending a church that encourages responsibility in its youth. But Hal?

It's not that he's stupid, or that he doesn't have good intentions. His IQ tests always come back way above normal, and his intentions are always excellent. But more and more he has been reminding me of what my grandmother used to say the road to hell was paved with.

There are times his conduct is normal, even exemplary. But then there are those other times—such as the day I came home and found Hal industriously waxing the kitchen floor with a can of Karo syrup because he wanted to help me and he hadn't bothered to read the label (and, as he virtuously pointed out to me while I screamed, the Johnson's Paste Wax was in the same size can), or when he was frantically running the football to his own goal line in a junior high championship game—when we are a little curious about just what is ticking around in that gray matter he calls his brain.

If Hal's less than adequately coherent note could be accepted as accurate, they had a ride all the way to Los Alamos. I wasn't altogether sure what they intended to eat on the way, but Hal—even at his worst—is enterprising. Also he has—or had—a bank account.

I tend to make decisions in cars. I remember that Harry and I were on our way to the library when we decided to adopt our first minority baby, who turned out to be Vicky, and we were on our way to the grocery store when we decided to ask for Becky (we'd read about her in the newspaper; her natural mother had abandoned her in a garbage can), and we were on our way back from a movie—about Korea—when we first started thinking about the baby who turned out to be Hal. I was driving to a doughnut shop when I finally made up my mind to answer that help wanted ad from the police department—the one that has had such a large effect on the last sixteen years of my life.

Of course I was in a car when I decided to marry Harry, but that was a long time ago and a story I don't exactly want to tell.

So by the time I reached Donna's house I knew what I was going to do. I was going to fly to Los Alamos and snatch that pair of yahoos home by the hair of their heads, that's what I was going to do. Of course I was going to. Who else could? Harry couldn't; he had a broken leg. Donna couldn't; as a single parent with house payments and a lot of other bills, she couldn't afford to take time off. But I was already into time off.

Yeah. I was already off work for several months because I was on medical leave because I was going to have a baby soon. Very, very soon, the doctor had assured me last time I went in. I really had a lot of business flying to Los Alamos. I'd be lucky if they let me on the plane.

That was what Donna told me. Not that she could come up with a better idea. Besides, as I said and Donna had to agree with me, the idea was bound to have been Hal's to begin with, not Lorie's, so it made sense for me to be the one—

That was what Harry told me. But he had the same problem Donna did—he couldn't think of anything except let them get home on their own, which he agreed didn't sound too smart either.

That's what my doctor would have told me, only I carefully didn't ask him.

That's what my mother told me, especially when we found out you can't fly to Los Alamos. You fly to Albuquerque and drive to Los Alamos, and it takes four to six hours, depending on how fast you drive and how many times you stop to pee, which when you're pregnant is frequently.

Oh, I could get a commuter flight from Albuquerque to Los Alamos, but I was going to have to rent a car anyway, and besides that, I might—probably would—get to New Mexico before the kids did, and—

Somewhere during this discussion, Harry said something like, "Oh, hell," and reminded me that since he'd now been off work more than thirty days his insurance had paid off the Visa card, but it certainly wouldn't pay for any more charges I happened to put on it.

I told him I knew that. And I told him I'd set our home telephone so that it would forward all calls right to his hospital bed. To which he said, "Oh, hell" again before telling me to take care of myself.

That was Saturday afternoon. It was Monday before I flew out. Obviously. We had to allow them time to get there.

THE ALBUQUERQUE AIRPORT terminal is under construction. I asked the girl at the Avis counter how long it had been that way, and she answered, "Forever." While the printer chattered out my contract, she added, "They've promised to be through in two more years. And if you believe that I've got this nice parcel of land on the moon I'd be glad to sell you."

She did tell me she figured it would be worth it when it was done, it was just that she was awfully tired of orange barrels. She then directed me to the place I was supposed to get the car—past the orange barrels, to the right, past some more orange barrels, through some more orange barrels, to the right again, and it would be in space 73.

Some airports have courtesy buses to take you to your rental car. This one did not. It wasn't really very far, though, or at least it would not be very far if you were not eight months plus pregnant, wearing high-heel shoes (in retrospect I haven't the faintest idea why I was wearing high-heel shoes), and lugging along a fair-size suitcase, a carry-on bag, and a purse large enough to be a bed for a cocker spaniel.

I did not, of course, wear my shoulder holster or gun on the airplane. I have better sense than that. It was packed in my luggage, which was why my luggage, which otherwise could have ridden with me on the plane (at least it could have if they hadn't started cracking down on too much carry-on luggage), had to go in the baggage compartment, which in turn was why I had just had to spend a good half hour waiting at the little carousel for my suitcase, complete with gun and holster, to get off the plane. It takes a lot longer for suitcases to get off planes than it does people.

At least the orange barrels were easy to find.

They certainly were easy to find, I thought grimly, as I managed to maneuver my way onto the highway. They were everywhere. It certainly must be lucrative to be a manufacturer of orange barrels in the state of New Mexico. I could only assume that every street, highway, and byway in Albuquerque was under construction or repair, all at the same time, and the orange barrels were there so that if you got lost because your road was full of orange barrels you could find it easily enough later by following more orange barrels.

I gave up the idea of stopping in Albuquerque. I'd have liked to, normally, because it's really a pretty town despite the orange barrels, and I've heard the people there are friendly, again despite the orange barrels, which certainly must be wearing on the nerves. But I was half-bilious from the too-sweet airplane food and too-stuffy airplane atmosphere, and I wanted to keep driving for a while.

I stopped at a cafeteria in the outskirts of Santa Fe for lunch, and then drove on. I'd never been in northern New Mexico before; every trip that had taken me through the state at all had taken me so far south I could see the mountains of northern Mexico on the southern horizon. To my mind, New Mexico was composed of sand and cactus and highways that stretch on and on forever and ever.

Northern New Mexico isn't. It is dry, but not desert, for a while, and you drive along rolling hills that let you forget you're about seven thousand feet above sea level and headed higher. After a while the land gets less and less dry looking, until suddenly, almost without noticing the transition, you're driving up mountain roads in a dense pine forest.

Now, I have no objections to pine trees. They grow a lot in East Texas, about two hundred miles east of Fort Worth, and I've seen them before, although I've got to admit that too many trees make me feel just a little bit claustrophobic.

No, the problem is mountains.

I hate driving in mountains. I loathe driving in mountains. All right, I admit it, I'm absolutely terrified of driving in mountains.

It didn't help any that the infant on the interior was picking that moment to practice his/her gymnastics, or that I was having what my obstetrician had told me were "practice contractions" that I'd keep having off and on until I was ready to deliver.

So there I was, inching up a mountain road at about twelve miles an hour in a very nice car that could happily have taken those roads at seventy-five if the speed limit permitted, while it felt like the Sells-Floto circus was practicing in my interior and cars were swooping around me at sixty and seventy, some of them honking indignantly but most of them obviously pitying me for the flatlander I certainly must be.

I couldn't help it. Shotguns I can manage, if I have to, though I sort of don't like them, especially when I'm looking at the north end of a northbound one, but mountain roads I cannot handle at all.

I kept telling myself I should be all right; this road was really too wide for me to fall off of. In fact it was several lanes wide; how wide I really don't know because I was far too busy shaking to be able to count, but anyway it was certainly better than it must have been back in the days when World War II was in progress and everybody at Los Alamos had the same post office box and some mail-order firm decided some idiot was playing a practical joke, because they'd already shipped 250 copies of their mail-order catalog to that box and they certainly weren't going to ship any more.

Oh, well. At least I knew a little more than I'd known a day earlier about how Hal and Lorie were managing. When I checked Harry's pickup truck, I found a few things missing from the camper—a few things like Hal's backpack and sleeping bag and Harry's backpack and sleeping bag (presumably for Lorie's use), Hal's canteen and Harry's canteen, Harry's water purification kit, and a small supply of dehydrated food. By the time I'd figured all that out I was telling myself I should be grateful they'd decided to hitchhike instead of taking Harry's truck, which for all I knew Hal might have decided to do if he'd been able to lay his hands on a gasoline credit card, which fortunately he had not been able to.

I should have been grateful but I was not. Everybody's heard tales of hitchhikers being murdered and/or assaulted, and cops hear even more such tales. My imagination, always a little hyperactive, was running wild. Hal and Lorie both dead somewhere in the desert. Hal dead and Lorie being raped. Hal and Lorie locked in the trunk of some sadist's car while the sadist decided what to do next.

I tried to force my imagination into more sensible patterns. Hal knocking out the evil assailant and escaping with Lorie. I couldn't make myself believe that one. Into more sensible possibilities. Hal and Lorie going all the way to Los Alamos in the truck of some nice family man who showed them pictures of his grandchildren while they were stopped to eat. Hal and Lorie wandering happily around a museum.

My imagination did not behave.

I arrived in Los Alamos about three-thirty in the afternoon, and the first thing I discovered was that there were two museums. One was right off the main road through town; the other, attached to the laboratory complex, involved going on another road and across a big bridge over a canyon and then to the right or maybe it was to the left, because I was get-

ting highly confused by this time and the elderly man
giving me directions was waving both arms at once
and seemed even more confused than I was.

The first museum was nearer.

It was a small one, dedicated mainly to local rather
than military history, and it had a registry book, the
kind where all visitors are supposed to sign their
names and their home towns. I immediately hit pay
dirt, because right there, just a few lines above my
own signature, were two others: *Harold Ralston*
(gad, he's getting formal, I thought—usually I see
that name only on his birth certificate and report
card) and *Laura Hankins, Fort Worth, Texas*. And
on the space for comments—well, never mind. It was
current teenage slang. The best that I could inter-
pret, it meant they liked the exhibits.

So they'd gotten here safely. That was something.
The next question was, What was I going to do about
finding them?

The book was dated, so I could tell they'd been
here sometime today. I couldn't be too far behind
them.

I couldn't be too far behind them, and I'd been
sitting down far too long and needed to stretch my
legs, and besides that, as I was signing the guest book
the elderly attendant wandered discreetly into a dis-
creet room she apparently intended to remain in for

a while. Clearly, the omens meant me to look around.

So I took about five minutes to wander around the museum, which was a very nice one that told me far more than I really wanted to know about Los Alamos as a community as it had been when I was a baby in Fort Worth and almost nobody knew that up here in this beautiful forest scientists were creating the very first of a new and unbelievably devastating kind of bomb.

Finally I went back to the reception area to find that the elderly woman had returned to her post in the gift shop. I identified myself and pulled out my badge. It rarely impresses people in Fort Worth, probably because they've seen plenty of Fort Worth police officers, but this old lady's eyes widened. "My, you're a long way from home," she informed me, and asked what I was doing.

From the avid look on her face, she must be expecting some sort of lurid explanation about murderers or spies or something equally exotic. I wasn't up to indulging her imagination. "I'm hunting a couple of runaway teenagers," I said. "You might have seen them—they signed the guest book today. A Korean-looking boy, very tall, and a girl about five-four, brown hair, blue eyes." I produced a photograph, Hal and Lorie together at a recent Western dance at school, and the woman peered at it.

"My, he's a big one," she said. "I surely would have remembered him. But I didn't come on until one—this is a volunteer project, you know."

"Oh, is it really?" I said, feeling rather as if I were being expected to make conversation at an afternoon tea. No, of course I didn't know this was a volunteer project. Why should I know?

But of course she didn't think I knew. She was just, in her own way, being polite. So I would have to go on being polite as well.

"Yes, and I don't come on until one. On Friday, that is. Friday's my day, you know."

"I see. Well, who—"

"Now, let me think. Fanny was here all morning, usually she's just here two hours but Ava was sick and so Fanny came in for her, too and—"

"Is there any way we could reach Fanny and ask her?"

"Well, now let me think—"

After a little more dithering, the volunteer—who still hadn't told me her name—managed to locate a telephone list. For all the good that did. Fanny—whoever Fanny was—did not answer her telephone.

"Well, thanks for trying," I said resignedly, and got a new set of directions to the other museum.

The other museum did not have a guest book. It did, however, have guards—a lot of them. We aren't going to let the Russians steal the secret of how the first atomic bomb was made and what it looked like in mockup, that is at least we aren't going to let them steal it without us knowing about it. The guards weren't really doing anything; they were just sort of there.

On sober second thought, it dawned on me they probably weren't there to guard against spies, especially in view of the fact that nothing would have been in the museum until it was cleared for public viewing; rather, they were most likely there in case of peace demonstrations and that sort of thing. They hadn't, I suspected, always been quite as successful as one would hope; one exhibit bore the marks of a splash of yellow paint.

Guards, being professionals, have at least semireasonable memories.

Yes, one of them did remember Hal and Lorie—remembered them both, largely because they'd asked permission to leave their backpacks and bedrolls by the front door. They'd both looked tired, and Lorie had gone and spent a lot of time in the women's rest room while Hal wandered around and looked at exhibits. When Lorie came out she looked as if she might have been crying, and Hal put his arm around her very protectively and they went out and sat on the grass for a long time before they trudged off down the road.

And that had been just a little before noon. They were almost four hours ahead of me.

That was more than I expected. Hal, at home, tends to be a late riser; he's rarely sane before ten-thirty or eleven. But I should have remembered that on camping trips he leaps up and kicks the sun out of bed. Of course here and now he'd be on his camping schedule, not his school schedule.

So now it was time to call for assistance. I could call the Los Alamos Police Department. I could call the sheriff's office of whatever county this was in. I could call the highway patrol or whatever they call it in New Mexico.

There was just one problem. In four hours they could be just about anywhere. If they were walking, they'd be at the most about twenty miles away, probably a lot less in view of their looking tired, of Lorie's reported crying.

On the other hand, if they'd found a ride they could be back in Albuquerque. Or off on any little side trip they'd decided to make before going home. Or, depending on the direction they'd taken, all the way out of the state.

I went and checked into a motel. I called Harry. He hadn't heard from them. I called Donna. She hadn't heard from them.

And then I called the sheriff's office.

THE TELEPHONE WOKE ME out of an unusually sound sleep—the change of altitude had me feeling totally wiped out—and for a moment I was so disoriented I couldn't find the telephone.

Then I remembered that I was in a motel in Los Alamos, and the telephone was across the room on that dresser thing all motels seem to have. I got up and made my way through the dark to the telephone, which I located by its little orange light, and answered.

"Deb?" It was Harry. "I've heard from Hal. Or rather, about Hal. He's in Las Vegas."

I was instantly wide awake. "Nevada?" I wailed. "How'd they get to—"

"Las Vegas, New Mexico," Harry interrupted. "You didn't let me finish."

"Where the heck is Las Vegas, New Mexico?" I demanded.

"Deb, would you, for cryin' out loud, let me finish?" Harry yelled. "I don't know where Las Vegas, New Mexico, is; I've never even heard of it. You're the one in New Mexico; look on a map and find it."

"Oh, I'll find it," I said grimly, "and then I will drive over there and strangle Hal with my bare hands before I bring the pair of them home."

"Well, good luck," Harry said, "because you're going to have to get him out of jail first."

"Sure, vagrancy," I said resignedly, wondering what the bond was going to be, and Harry said, "Not quite, Deb."

"What do you mean, *not quite?*"

"Deb, this police chief that called me said he's holding Hal on suspicion of murder."

TWO

ADULTS ARE NO LONGER jailed "on suspicion" of anything. Courts have gotten somewhat sticky on requiring such little niceties as properly executed warrants telling who is to be arrested and on what grounds. But a juvenile who is not at least approximately where he is supposed to be, doing approximately what he is supposed to be doing, becomes by definition a "status offender." And a status offender can, with very few exceptions, be held just about as long as anybody wants to hold him, on just about whatever pretext anybody wants to use.

Of course I telephoned Las Vegas.

Of course the person I talked with—a female named Vargas and judging from the noise in the background I guessed she was a dispatcher—said, politely but firmly, "I'm sorry, ma'am, I can't possibly give out that information over the telephone."

Okay, calm down, Deb Ralston, I told myself. I've been in her position, and I wouldn't give out that information over the telephone either.

Still in my underwear—I had somehow neglected to pack a nightgown—I sat down on the bed, took a deep breath, and looked at my watch. Just after five A.M. Mountain Time is six A.M. Central Time, which is the time I usually get up, so I ought to be at least halfway beginning to approximate sanity. Use some common sense, I told myself. Be reasonable. Whatever stupid thing Hal had done—and knowing Hal, I was prepared to guess it could be just about anything as long as it was really stupid he certainly had not really murdered anyone. That was beyond the bounds of possibility. Eccentric—if one can use the word for a sixteen-year-old—he is; violent or mean, he is not.

Heading for my suitcase, which was open beside the telephone, I rather fuzzily dug for maps.

No maps.

I checked my handbag and carry-on bag before remembering that I had left the maps in the right-hand front seat of the rented Ford Escort. And obviously I was not going out to the car in my present attire.

The heck with it, I thought; whatever Hal did, he certainly didn't kill anybody. (I was going to go on telling myself that.) There was clearly some kind of error. I would get there, get it straightened out, and that would be the end of it, except that Hal, once I got him home, might find himself grounded for about the next ten years. In the meantime, it

wouldn't hurt him to cool his young tail in the slammer a few more hours. In fact, I'd be inclined to say
he deserved it, after all he'd put Harry and me and
Donna through.

So saying—not very convincingly—I went to take
a shower. I put on clean clothes. I ate breakfast. And
then I left for Las Vegas. (The fact that I was on the
road by approximately 6:45 A.M. may be taken as
some indication that I was not quite as calm as I was
trying to tell myself I was, but that's immaterial.)

According to the map I had studied while I was
eating, it would be about 120 miles from Los Alamos (The Poplars, in case you don't speak Spanish)
to Las Vegas (The Meadows). I could go from Los
Alamos to Santa Fe to Las Vegas, or I could go from
Los Alamos to Chimayo to Rodarte to Mora to Las
Vegas. Either way I would be driving over the Sangre
de Cristo Mountains. Oh shit, I thought, remembering myself inching up from Santa Fe the day before.
A hundred miles at 12 miles an hour, I'd be lucky to
get there in one day, provided of course I didn't get
run over or shot by some irate motorist stuck behind
me for 20 or 30 or 40 miles.

If I went through Santa Fe I'd have main roads all
the way; if I went by way of Chimayo, et cetera, I'd
have secondary roads. But on the other hand if I
went through Santa Fe I'd be hitting the state capi-

tal at rush hour, which could cost me two hours. I decided to chance the secondary roads, even though the idea of secondary roads over mountains didn't exactly light up my galaxy. Mentally gritting my teeth, I checked out of the motel.

Surprise, surprise. A pleasant surprise for a change. Most of the time, I could not have told I was in the mountains at all, except for that extraordinary clarity the air gets in high altitudes. It was almost like driving through East Texas. Pine trees, almost the same except that the needles were shorter and somehow tuftier. Undergrowth very much the same. The same red clay, only slightly more orange here, the same fantastically shaped pebbles of iron ore, even the same sunlit glades with the occasional grazing deer, except that instead of East Texas's small, dainty white-tails these were big mule deer or often elk.

Most of the way I was driving through dense forest on a two-lane highway, meeting absolutely nobody except, every now and then, a mountain biker maybe in training for the Olympics. Ordering myself to calm down had done no good whatever, but this peaceful landscape really did settle my nerves. I'd be glad to stay here permanently, I thought, until I remembered the altitude and the latitude and thought about nasty things like twelve-foot snowdrifts all winter long. Even now, in late March, I was seeing frequent large patches of unmelted snow under shading tree limbs and on the lee sides of hills.

And then, quite suddenly, I was out of the forest and looking down a long hill onto meadowland, with a sparkling lake (Storrie Lake, according to my map) off ahead to my right. I was still about twenty miles out of Las Vegas, but twenty miles in the country isn't like twenty miles in the city. It was a little short of 8:45 when I arrived in Las Vegas, which turned out to be divided roughly by the Gallinas River into two parts, which seemed, depending on whom I talked with, to be Las Vegas and East Las Vegas, or Old Town and New Town, or Hispanic and Anglo (except that lots of Hispanics live in the Anglo section and lots of Anglos live in the Hispanic section). With all that useful information, it only took me an extra twenty-five minutes to locate the police station, which turned out to be in Anglo/New/East Las Vegas as opposed to Hispanic/Old/Las Vegas. The building was sort of beigeish and looked about eighty years old, which, for this town I'd now been informed billed itself as "The Other Las Vegas," seemed to be fairly new. In Old Town I had already been shown an apartment building on the roof of which, I was assured, General Whatever-his-name-was had stood, in eighteen-forty-whenever-it-was, to announce to the citizens of New Mexico (very few of whom were in earshot) that they were now citizens of the United States. In general, I had also been informed, the change in government had made little difference in anybody's life.

I could believe that. What I found it hard to believe was that anybody had found it necessary to explain all that to me when all I had asked was how to get to the police station. I could explain it only as an extreme local patriotism, which would have been more heartwarming if I had been less worried.

The building—the apartment building, not the police station, which I hadn't located yet—faced a very interesting little public square with a sort of gazebo or bandstand where a number of people, including two uniformed police officers, seemed to be very busy.

The police station was about eleven blocks away, near the chamber of commerce, which in turn was near the Rough Riders Museum. In fact, I discovered to my chagrin that I had already passed it several times while trying to sort out the directions given me by various extremely helpful, extremely enthusiastic, but more or less poorly informed citizens.

The next fifteen minutes I spent sitting on a straight chair in a sort of a little anteroom, facing the front door, with a glassed-in dispatch booth (bullet-proof glass, I guessed) in front of me to my right and various other doors leading off in various other directions, including one just behind me and to my left that was labeled CHIEF'S OFFICE. Finally the girl in the dispatch booth, who apparently served also as receptionist and desk officer, told me Chief Salazar would see me now. The door behind me buzzed. Wise in the ways of doors that buzz, I opened it fast before it had time to change its mind.

Chief Alberto Salazar was sitting behind a very neat desk with a nameplate. On a wall behind his head were several framed certificates that informed me that Alberto Rafael Salazar had a B.S. in law enforcement from the University of New Mexico, a law degree from the University of New Mexico College of Law, and a certificate from the FBI National Academy, that superduper police school that only the best and most experienced law enforcement officers are ever invited to attend.

I was suitably impressed.

Alberto Rafael Salazar was about two inches taller than my five-two. Normally he might outweigh me by a pound or two, but right now I (complete with passenger) definitely outweighed him. He had straight black hair and almond-shaped brown eyes and dark red-khaki skin.

I am aware that the Hispanic population of northern New Mexico is far more likely to be pure Spanish than the Mestizo-Creole of Mexico. But at a glance, I'd say Alberto Rafael Salazar was at least three-quarters Hopi or some other kind of Pueblo Indian.

I wasn't, of course, standing and staring while figuring out all of this; I was absorbing impressions while getting out my ID and handing it across the desk. Salazar looked at it, returned it to me, sat back companionably, and said, "Now, Mrs. Ralston, how may I help you?"

"You have my son and his girlfriend in jail," I said. He frowned, looked puzzled, and started sorting through papers, while I went on talking. "I need to get the problem straightened out and get them on home."

"Your son's Harold Ralston?" he asked, looking at me with the puzzled expression people usually get after seeing me introduced as Hal's mother.

I nodded. "Hal. We call him Hal. And before you ask, yes, he's adopted."

"After seeing you, I would sort of think he would have to be. But I'm afraid getting him out of jail isn't going to be all that easy. Besides that, we don't have his girlfriend at all."

"No? Then where is she?"

"What's her name? Can you describe her?"

"Laura Hankins," I said, and handed the picture from the Western dance across the desk. "About five-four, brown hair, blue eyes. Fifteen years old."

He shook his head. "It's not her, then."

"What's not her?" I interrupted.

"The victim."

And it was not until that moment that it had crossed my conscious mind that the victim might *be* Lorie. In fact, I hadn't quite let it into my mind that for Hal to be held on suspicion of murder, there had to be a victim. And then the connection clicked in my mind: the crowd on the old town plaza. I should have realized what was happening when I saw that crowd. Someone was working a crime scene, and a lot of people were watching.

"Can we start at the beginning?" I asked, feeling more feeble than I probably sounded. "Just what is it that Hal's supposed to have done?"

"The beginning," Salazar shuffled through papers again. "About midnight last night one of my patrol officers noticed a couple of people apparently asleep on the ground by the bandstand in the town plaza. Well, that's against the law, of course, but they had sleeping bags and hadn't built a fire or done anything dumb like that, so he decided just to leave them alone and notify the oncoming shift. They were checked several times during the night. Then long about four A.M. another car went by and saw a very tall figure walking around and saw him bend over the other sleeping bag and then straighten fast. And he just—had a feeling. The officer, I mean. He just had a feeling. You know what I mean?"

I nodded. An experienced cop gets that kind of feeling. A rookie doesn't. It usually takes three or four years of experience.

"So he pulled over to check them out. The male who was walking around had blood on his hands and on his clothes. The female on the ground had been hacked to pieces with some kind of butcher knife or hunting knife. There was a bloody hunting knife lying on the ground nearby. The male said it belonged to his father. The officer asked where his father was and he said his father was in the hospital and he— Lady, are you all right? You're looking some kind of pale."

"I'm all right. But the girl—"

"Is not your Laura Hankins. The boy said he'd never seen her before yesterday and didn't know who she was except a first name. April. He kept asking where Lorie was. He said April was in Lorie's sleeping bag and Lorie was gone. He was pretty hysterical—kept trying to break away from the officers and yelling for Lorie—and we put him in a cell to quiet him down and wound up calling a doctor to come out and give him a sedative. I just checked on him and he's still asleep. Now, if you want, I'll go and wake him up, but I'd say let him sleep."

"Let him sleep," I agreed. "But Lorie—"

"I gave you all we know about Lorie," he said.

"Chief Salazar, she's fifteen years old. Her mother's a police officer and the widow of another police officer."

"Mrs. Ralston—Detective Ralston—I can't give you what I don't have. I'd offer to put a lookout on her but there's one already—we put a partial on early this morning, from what we had, and NCIC kicked back a complete. Yours?"

"Mine," I acknowledged. And how often had I been on his side of the desk, feeling the frustration he must be feeling now. He was right. No matter who Laura Hankins was, no matter how important Laura Hankins might be to Hal or Donna or me or anybody else, he couldn't give me Laura Hankins if he didn't have Laura Hankins.

And, on the basis of what he'd told me, he couldn't give me Hal either. Not right now. Not until he knew a lot more about what had happened last night in the plaza than he knew at this moment.

He was still watching me. "Mrs. Ralston," he asked now, "you ever seen a homicide?"

"Deb," I said. "You might as well call me Deb. Everybody else does. Yes, Chief Salazar, in sixteen years I've probably seen hundreds of homicides. And for the last three years that's been about all I've worked."

He nodded. "That's what I figured. That you've seen them, anyway, not necessarily that you've worked them. Well, if you're up to it, you can do you and me both a big favor. Thing is, in Las Vegas we get at the most about two homicides a year, and they're usually nothing—you know, the kind where you've got fourteen witnesses and by the time the first car gets there the killer's sitting on the curb crying."

"You're asking me to help?"

"It's unusual," he said, "but look, you want your boy back, and there's no way in hell I can just hand him over to you. Not now, not the way it looks now. The way I see it, the only way he's going to walk is if someone else did it and we can prove it. Now, you've worked a hell of a lot more killings than I have. But are you sure you're up to working this one?"

"I'm up to it," I said.

"And if you help work it and find out he did do it, then what are you going to do?"

"It won't happen," I said, "because he didn't do it."

ALMOST HALF THE TOWN plaza was roped off with uniformed police guards standing by, and, as usual for any crime scene, about half the town was watching avidly from the other side of the ropes. This time they had plenty to watch. Salazar had told me on the way over that a lab crew was coming up from Santa Fe, the state capital, and in the meantime nothing had been moved.

In this case, nothing meant literally nothing.

At a guess, I'd say that April—whoever April was going to turn out to be; the girl in Harry's sleeping bag anyway—was around seventeen or eighteen. But it was hard to say for sure. Her light brown or dark blond hair was now matted with drying blood; her brown eyes, half-open, stared sightlessly at the sky. Her face was pallid; as she'd apparently nearly bled dry, there wouldn't be much postmortem lividity, and rigor mortis hadn't set in yet. She was quite a lot taller than Lorie, around five-seven or five-eight, but probably around the same weight. She was naturally thin, or she'd dieted carefully, or—quite possibly— she was anorexic.

Somebody would get the joyous task of counting, and mapping, the knife wounds. I was glad that someone almost certainly would not be me. The sleeping bag, unzipped all the way, seemed to have no cuts on it, but I didn't want to guess at the condition of the body inside the blood-soaked—but obviously expensive—jeans and silk shirt she was wearing. Her face and arms also had multiple wounds, and there were defense wounds on her hands. Which said she'd been awake, she'd tried to fight.

Her bare feet were small, with very high arches, and she was wearing something on her left ankle that at first glance I thought was a wristwatch. I bent to look closer. It wasn't a wristwatch. It was some kind of woven leather band.

"I thought you'd notice that," Salazar said behind me. "What do you suppose it is?"

I shook my head. I couldn't guess what it was; I'd never seen anything quite like it before. "She must have fought," I said. "She must have screamed."

I didn't put the rest of my thought into words, but I went on thinking it. Did Hal hear her scream? If he did, what did he do about it?

If he didn't hear her scream, why didn't he? And that was the real question, because if Hal had awakened to see this going on he would be lying here too, or else the killer would, because there was no way Hal would not have fought if he'd awakened to see this going on.

The presumed murder weapon, a large hunting knife I had no trouble recognizing, lay a few feet away. Harry had made it himself from a kit, some green Plexiglas from the canopy of a crashed jet, and some gimp and glue and beads. It had to be unique.

It was on the ground between the two sleeping bags, not far from a pair of expensive-looking, but somewhat muddy, multicolored sandals. The beads, the gimp, and the green Plexiglas were almost uniformly coated with blood, thick coagulating blood, as was the blade. But in addition, there were a few fat globules clinging to the blade. The blood would have splashed freely; it could have splattered onto a knife just lying on the ground, or a knife someone had drawn to use to fight back. But the fat globules said this was the murder weapon, period and no room for doubt, because if that knife had gone far enough into somebody else to collect those fat globules, that somebody else wouldn't have gone very far afterward.

I knew Salazar knew that. Salazar knew I knew that. He of course asked me if it was my husband's knife, since Hal had already told him it was, and of course I had to tell him Hal was right, which in turn brought forth a brief explanation of why it was me, rather than my husband, who had come tracking our errant son to bring him home.

Salazar expressed sympathy and properly went on about his business, while I went on about mine, which at the moment seemed to consist of examining this crime scene.

Blood had splattered the white paint of the bandstand and the winter-brown grass just starting to green for spring, and blood had splashed Hal's sleeping bag and Harry's backpack. Hal's backpack wasn't there. Had it gone with Lorie, wherever Lorie went?

Examining the few things already out of the pack—I very properly wasn't touching anything until I was told the lab was through—I asked, "Are you officers sure there were only two people camping here?" Because why had Lorie left? And how long ago? Had Lorie wakened to the sound of April screaming, seen what was happening, grabbed her pack (or Hal's pack that she was using?), and run? Was she even now hiding out somewhere in the European-style rabbit-warren streets some parts of Las Vegas Old Town had? Had she gotten out onto the highway and hitched a ride she hoped would take her home?

Or if not, if she'd left before the killing, why hadn't she taken the sleeping bag she'd certainly been using? (Unless I was very wrong indeed, and April had been sharing a sleeping bag with Hal—not an impossibility at their age, no matter what I would like to think.)

But if she'd been awakened by April's screams, how had April gotten into her sleeping bag?

Had Lorie and Hal been sharing a sleeping bag? Or Lorie and April? Or April and Hal?

One more sinister possibility remained, and it was to shunt my mind away from the possibility—probability—that whoever had killed April now had Lorie. And I began to wonder again where April had come from anyway.

I asked Salazar. He reminded me that last night— well, this morning—Hal had been in no condition to tell anybody anything, and the best they'd been able to get from him so far was her first name. That had taken some doing, and it might or might not be her real first name at all; she wasn't far off the age when kids all want to change their names. Of course they'd run her on NCIC with what they had—first name, rough physical description—but nobody seemed at the moment to be missing April.

Which might mean she was not named April, or it might mean nobody had noticed yet that she was missing, or—just maybe—it might mean the people who ought to be missing her were dead somewhere themselves.

Because even on a corpse, usually, you can tell a little something about background. April's slashed fingers had long nails, neatly manicured with pale pink nail polish. April's jeans and shirt definitely had come from a store where I couldn't afford to shop, and April's tennis bracelet hadn't been bought from an advertisement on a back page of the *National Enquirer*. April's soft blond hair hadn't been cut in a small-town beauty college, and April's sandals hadn't come from a K-mart. All of which said that somebody, somewhere, ought to be missing April.

I judged it was time to go wake up Hal and ask him a few questions.

Salazar pushed his hat to the back of his head and nodded wearily. "Might as well take him something to eat," he said. "He drink coffee? He's gonna need something to wake him up."

THREE

WITH THE LARGEST Coke I could find in Las Vegas, and a couple of hamburgers, we went to wake up Hal. He was even less coherent than his usual incoherent morning self, but after whatever sedatives they'd given him at four A.M., or whenever it was, that was probably to be expected.

"Hi, Mom," he said sleepily. He sat up—in a shirt with blood on it, in jeans with blood on them; why hadn't Salazar taken those clothes away from him and put him into coveralls? He rubbed fretfully at his eyes and then, stretching with his arms behind him, he looked around. His eyes widened, and he scrambled out of the metal jail bunk, managing not to bump his head on the one above it. "Mom! What are you doing here?"

"What do you think I'm doing here?" I demanded, and put the Coke and hamburgers down so I could hug him. "Hal, how could you—"

"Mom, I didn't—"

"—be so stupid—"

"But Mom—"

"—as to take off by yourself like that, just you and Lorie?"

"Oh, that." He sat back down, rather abruptly. "Yeah, I did do that."

"What did you think I was talking about?"

"That girl. Mom, did you see that girl?" Corpses are nothing new to me, but they don't fall into Hal's normal galaxy, and he was looking more than a little bit green.

"I'm afraid I did. Hal, who in the world was she?"

He shrugged. "Just a girl. She said her name was April. Hey, Mom, where's Lorie?"

"Now we were hoping you'd be able to help us figure that out," Salazar said, behind me.

"Well, I don't know, I told you last night I don't know. She was there when I went to sleep. Somebody ought to be able to find her. Unless—"

"Unless what?" I asked.

He scrambled to his feet again, a look of horror building on his face. "Mom, do you s'pose who-ever . . . did that . . . took her? Took Lorie?"

"I expect Lorie saw what was going on and ducked out and hid. She'll turn up eventually."

"You really think so?"

I nodded, feeling guilty. The truth was that I didn't really think so. If she were coming out of hiding she'd have done so already; the square was swarming with cops, and even the most timid shrinking violet ought to feel safe by now. Lorie has never been what I would want to call timid. So Hal's suggestion wasn't just a possibility; it was a probability. But there were other possibilities, not all of them quite that bad.

"I'll be helping Chief Salazar," I said, "and we're going to need a lot of help from you."

"What kind of help?"

"Need to ask you some questions," Salazar said, still behind me, "and we need some answers. A whole damn lot of answers."

"Oh, that kind of help," Hal said. "When Mom said a lot of help, I thought—"

Salazar moved restlessly. "So, are you ready to come out and answer questions?"

"Uh—can I wait a minute?"

"Wait a minute for what?" Salazar demanded.

Hal wriggled a little, and Salazar repeated the question. Hal looked embarrassed, and then blurted out, "I've got to pee."

"By all means pee," Salazar said, and led me back to his office. Pointing me to a chair, he said, "I'll let him take a shower. You can wait here."

It was nearly half an hour later before Hal, in jail coveralls with his hair damp and tousled, appeared.

Salazar, following right behind him, told him to sit down and he sat, placing his now-cold hamburgers and half-consumed Coke on the corner of Salazar's desk.

I am not used to seeing a chief of police personally conducting an investigation, much less escorting prisoners to take showers. But on the other hand I do not live in a small town. Salazar might—maybe—have two investigators. Certainly no more. He'd already told me he didn't have much experience working homicides. But most likely he was the only one in his department who had the appropriate training.

And he definitely was not stupid. If I hadn't already figured that out for myself, his first words to Hal would have told me. "I called Fort Worth," he said. "They tell me your mom's a pretty sharp cop."

As Hal was mumbling an indistinct reply around a mouthful of hamburger, I thought, So that's it. I'd wondered why he felt secure enough to leave me alone in his office. I wouldn't do that for a stranger, no matter what kind of credentials said stranger walked in with. Credentials are too easily forged.

No, that wasn't the reason. At least that wasn't the only reason. Salazar pointed up. "See that?" he said to Hal.

Hal looked up. So did I. "Yeah," Hal said. "So?"

"That's a camera," Salazar said. "When I push a button the dispatcher can see everything that's going on in this office. So you're going to behave yourself, right?"

"I was going to behave anyway," Hal protested. "When are you gonna push the button?"

"Oh, I did that a long time ago," Salazar said. His gaze slid enigmatically over me.

So—as I had sat in his office, resisting all impulses to open his case file and start reading his notes, a camera had been watching me. If I hadn't been who I said I was—if Fort Worth dispatch had been mistaken, or prompted to lie—it would have all been on videotape.

And of course there were no weapons at hand, and his desk and file drawers were locked. The only things I could have gotten at, other than that tempting file jacket, were police science textbooks and daily bulletins.

Canny man, this Salazar. And judging from the look on his face, he was following my thoughts about as well as if he were thinking them himself.

Hal, meanwhile, was reducing the hamburgers to crumbs. I waited until he could talk without spraying, and then asked, "Hal, what about it?"

"What about what?"

Salazar and I must have worn equal looks of disbelief, because Hal corrected himself at once. "I mean I know what about, but where do you want me to start?"

Salazar gestured at me.

"Start in Fort Worth," I said. "How'd you get here?"

"Oh. Well, we hitchhiked."

"I know—" I could hear my voice rising.

"Okay, okay, I mean we got a ride with this real nice guy."

"What real nice guy?"

"A driver. A truck driver. He drove this eighteen-wheeler and he was going to Albuquerque and he told us we could ride along with him only we'd have to buy our own food. He even let me drive some. Wow, Mom, that was great! There's so many gears!"

I could imagine that it was great. What I preferred not to imagine was a sixteen-year-old who's been driving an automobile for only about four months, usually under close supervision, barreling down the highway in control of however many tons it is of eighteen-wheeler.

But it would do no good at all to make mommy noises right now. "So you got to Albuquerque. Then what?"

"So then we got a ride to Santa Fe with this real nice guy."

"What real nice—"

"Well, I don't know. I mean I don't know his name, how'm I s'posed to know..."

"You ever hear of asking?"

"That wouldn't have been polite."

"So you got a ride to Santa Fe," Salazar put in, interrupting what was in the process of becoming a not-too-affectionate mother-son dialogue.

"Yeah, to the governor's palace. I mean not the now governor. It was this real old building with a great big porch, you know, and this guy we rode with, he had this real old pickup, but he had all this pretty jewelry and he was gonna sell the jewelry at the governor's palace."

This was making no sense at all to me, and my expression must have said so, because Salazar, who was slowly sliding down in his seat, said, "Indians are allowed to peddle jewelry in front of the old colonial governor's palace, which is now a museum. Go on, Hal."

"Okay, well, he said he was a Navajo. And his jewelry was real pretty. If I'd had enough money I would have bought Lorie some of it."

"He was a Navajo and his jewelry was pretty and he took you to Santa Fe. So how'd you get to Los Alamos?"

"Well, we found this place to sleep, this sort of a park, and then we sort of looked around Santa Fe in the morning—hey, how come practically all the houses have ladders up to the roof?"

"It's a custom," Salazar said. "As your mother asked, how'd you get to Los Alamos?"

"Well, we got this ride with this real nice—"

"Guy," I interrupted resignedly.

"Lady," Hal said reproachfully. "A real nice lady. She was going to work. She said a lot of people who work in Los Alamos live in Santa Fe. So Lorie asked her why she was just now going to work when it was almost lunchtime and she said she had an experiment she was watching. And she offered us a cigarette but we said no thank you."

I can't stand it when Hal puts on that air of great virtue. It usually means he's up to serious mischief and hopes the visible virtue will hide what else he's doing. In this case we already knew about the mischief, so maybe he thought the air of virtue would serve as a mitigating circumstance.

If he thought that he was very much mistaken.

But most likely he didn't think that at all. Most likely he wasn't even thinking that much. He was just remembering he's not allowed to smoke. The realization that what he had done was far more serious than smoking probably hadn't tippytoed into his brain yet.

But at least we now had them into Los Alamos. We were into Monday. Yesterday.

"So we went to this one museum," Hal said, "and then we were going to this other museum only we got kinda lost, and we walked and walked and then this real jerky guy in a Corvette made like he was gonna run over us and we had to run to get out of his way, and Lorie fell down, and then she started crying, and then she said her, uh, I mean she said—" He came to a dead halt.

"Said what, son?" Salazar prodded gently. And it was odd, because Hal was at least a foot taller than Salazar and by now Salazar had slid so far down in his chair, and put his feet up on his desk, that he was practically lying down, but even so there was no doubt whatever in anybody's mind that Salazar was in control in that room.

"She, uh, she said her period started," Hal disclosed, more bashfully than you would expect of a kid with two older sisters. "And so we found this store, and, uh, got some stuff and she went to a rest room. And she said she had cramps and I said why should she have cramps, she wasn't swimming, and she said not that kind of cramps, dummy, and I didn't know what she was talking about."

"With two sisters you don't know—"

"Oh. Oh, yeah, okay. That kind of cramps. Well, I just wasn't thinking."

"You frequently aren't thinking. Go on."

"So we got the people in the store to tell us how to get to this other museum. And then we went there and Lorie said she had to go to the rest room again, so she did, and she stayed there for ages, and I walked around and looked at everything and waited for Lorie, and finally she came out and she looked at a few things and then she said she wanted to go home, so we went outside and then she said she was tired and wanted to rest, and I said you wanta rest or you want to go home. And she said she wanted to rest and then go home. So we sat in the grass awhile and then we went out to what we thought was the main road, only it turned out it wasn't, and we found a ride with this guy—"

"Not a real nice guy?" I couldn't resist asking.

Hal glared at me. "No. He was drunk or something, only we didn't know it until we got in the car. And he was driving kind of crazy and he wouldn't stop and let us out, and then I noticed we weren't on the road to Santa Fe and I asked if this was another road to Santa Fe and he laughed and I asked where he was going, and he said we'd find out, and I could have jumped out of the car myself only every time he slowed up he grabbed hold of Lorie and I couldn't leave Lorie, and so—"

"So you were stuck," Salazar said.

"Yeah. I was stuck. We were stuck. And then he stopped on the side of the road and he started, you know, grabbing Lorie and I hit him and pulled Lorie out of the car and we grabbed our backpacks and he started to grab Lorie again and I pulled my knife on him, because, Mom, I know I'm not s'posed to fight, but I thought he was gonna, you know—"

"I have never told you not to defend yourself."

"But it was Lorie. He wasn't grabbing me."

"You are allowed to defend Lorie. But whose knife—"

"Oh. Yeah. Well, it's Dad's really, but I figured—" He stopped.

"You figured what?"

"Well, we had to—I mean I had to have some way to defend ourselves if we had to, on a trip like this, and I knew you wouldn't let me take a gun."

"Hal, I wouldn't even have let you take the trip, and you know that perfectly well."

"Well," Hal said, ignoring me, "well, anyway, I had Dad's knife. And it was pretty lucky I did. So he drove off real fast, and we were on this country road.

I mean it was nothing but the road and the pine trees, no other cars, no signs, no nothing. So Lorie was crying, and I asked if she was gonna sit on the side of the road and cry or if we were going to try to get home, and she started yelling at me and saying it was all my fault."

"So?" Salazar was still leaning back, apparently completely relaxed, with his hands folded behind his head. "Sounds to me as if she was right."

"Yeah, but she didn't have to say so."

"Ah, the perils of youth," Salazar said. "So how'd you get from point A to point B?"

"Huh?" Hal said.

"How'd you get to Las Vegas?"

Hal stared at Salazar. "We didn't go to Las Vegas. What would we want to go there for?"

"Hal, you're in Las Vegas," I said.

"No, I'm not. I mean, look, I know I'm crummy in geography, but I do know what state I'm in. I'm in New Mexico. Las Vegas is in Arizona."

It was Salazar's turn to look completely befuddled. I didn't blame him. Hal is hopeless in geography. Last fall, when my older daughter, Vicky, and her husband and baby left for Tulsa, Hal thought they were going to Oregon or Ohio.

When I get him home this time, I thought, I ought to make him memorize an atlas. That might keep him out of mischief for a day or two.

"The Las Vegas you're thinking of," I told him, "is in Nevada. Not Arizona."

"Oh. You sure?"

"Positive. But you are in another town, which as you rightly pointed out is in New Mexico, and which also is named Las Vegas."

"Oh. You sure?"

"You sound like a broken record. Yes, I'm sure."

Salazar, still with the dazed look on his face, uncurled long enough to hand him a business card. "If I don't know what town I'm chief of police of, I'm in some more kind of bad shape."

Hal studied the card. "Oh," he said finally. "Okay. Well, I didn't know."

"So now you know. And I want to know how you got here from wherever it was you got ditched."

"Oh. Well, Lorie finally quit crying, but we were real thirsty, and we didn't have much water left in our canteens because we forgot to fill them up in Los Alamos, but we drank what we had and then we just started walking down the road."

"Which way?" I asked.

"We know which way," Salazar said. "They got here. At least he got here."

"Not by walking. That'd be a minimum four-day hike."

Salazar shrugged. "True. So?"

"Well, we knew we'd come a long way from Los Alamos, and it was starting to get dark, so we thought—I thought—the next town might be closer the other way, so we walked the way the car had gone. And we came to this sign about a park, off to the left. So we talked about it, and we figured at least they'd have rest rooms and drinking fountains and maybe we could camp there overnight, and we still had like Tiger's Milk bars and stuff like that to eat, so we wouldn't get too hungry, and Lorie had her, well, you know, the stuff she needed. And—and so we went that way, and it was, oh, I don't know, maybe a couple of miles off the road and Lorie was getting real upset again, but then we got to the park and it had a little café sort of thing and so I was going to get Lorie a hamburger only the place turned out to be closed so I gave Lorie one of my Tiger's Milk bars and I figured that ought to make her feel better only it didn't."

"The ways of women are beyond comprehension," Salazar said to the ceiling. "So then what?"

"So I wanted to walk around, there were all these real wild ruins, and over on this cliff there was like this whole apartment house like, and there was this real groovy hole in the ground—''

"A real groovy hole in the ground?''

"An old kiva that's been excavated. Bandelier,'' Salazar said. He was no longer talking to the ceiling, at least not so far as I could tell; since he now had his eyes shut, I was a little vague about whom he was addressing. "Bandelier National Monument. That's where you were, right, Hal? That is where you were?''

"I guess. It started with a B, anyway.''

"So what time was this?''

"I don't know. It was about sundown.''

"Call it five-thirty, six, sundown this time of year?''

"I guess.''

"So at six o'clock yesterday evening you and Lorie were at Bandelier National Monument and at four o'clock this morning you were on the town square of Las Vegas with the body of a girl named April, who still hasn't gotten into the story at all, and Lorie was nowhere to be found. Sounds like a kinda busy ten hours. Was it?''

"Not very.''

"So what's that supposed to mean?'' Salazar came out of his sprawl, which I'd suspected was at least ninety percent feigned anyway, and sat straight up and looked at Hal.

"Just, not much happened."

"Then suppose you tell me what did happen."

"Well, we were at the park," Hal said.

"We got that far," Salazar reminded him.

"We asked this park guy, this guy in this green uniform—"

"A ranger?"

"A ranger, yeah. We asked him if we could camp there and he said yeah but it'd be as cold as, uh, he said it would be cold."

"As cold as what?" Salazar was determined to get all the details.

"As cold as a witch's tits in January," Hal said guiltily, and glanced at me.

"I've heard the phrase before," I assured him. "But he said that in front of Lorie?"

"No, just to me."

"But he did say you could camp there," Salazar prompted.

"Yeah."

"So why didn't you?"

"We were going to. I mean, I was going to. I mean—well, look, maybe I'd better explain."

"That sounds like a grand idea," I said. The infant on my interior, who had been asleep, abruptly woke up and began practicing gymnastics; between Hal on the exterior being impossible and Little Whosit on the interior being impossible, I was becoming exceedingly short of patience.

"Okay, well, I was walking around looking at things and I wanted to walk up to that apartment-like kind of thing I told you about on the cliff only it was getting dark and I figured Lorie wouldn't want to go with me because she was pretty tired and so, well, I didn't figure I ought to leave her alone after dark."

His reasoning, so far as it went, was excellent. However, it seemed the possibility of missing his footing climbing a cliff in the dark hadn't entered his mind at all. I should be grateful Lorie was with him.

"So I was just walking around looking at stuff, and then I went back to the buildings, you know, the rest room and gift shop and that little café sort of and that room where they sell books and stuff only it was closed, but anyhow Lorie was sitting on the ground talking to this girl."

"April?" Salazar asked.

"Yeah. Only I didn't know her name yet. But anyhow Lorie and this girl April were talking and I guess Lorie was crying again and April gave her some stuff."

"Gave her what stuff?"

"I don't know. Just some stuff to take. She said it would make her feel better."

"When you say 'stuff,' was it pills or what?"

"I don't know. I didn't see it. Just, Lorie said April gave her some stuff for cramps."

That, I thought, was just really truly extremely utterly informative. "Some stuff for cramps" could have been anything from aspirin, Midol, or Nuprin to hashish, crack, or LSD. You would figure a cop's kid would have better sense than to take "stuff" a stranger gave her in a park. But then you would figure a cop's kid—or, rather, three cops' two kids—would have better sense than to take off on a harebrained excursion like this to start with.

"Did you see Lorie take the stuff?" asked Salazar, whose mind was clearly following on the same tracks mine was.

"Uh-uh. She went in the rest room."

"So how'd she act when she came out of the rest room?"

"What do you mean, how'd she act? She just acted like Lorie."

Maybe Salazar and I just had nasty suspicious minds. Maybe April just gave Lorie some perfectly ordinary across-the-counter pain pills. Girls do things like that for each other. Even strangers.

Maybe.

But April's body hacked to pieces in the park in Lorie's sleeping bag said something very damned unordinary had happened that night, and Salazar—and I, but the job was primarily Salazar's—had to find out what and how and why.

"Okay, so April gave Lorie something for cramps and Lorie went in the rest room and took it and then what?" Salazar was completely calm, completely patient. He was going to get the truth out of Hal, and if he had to question Hal for a week to get it, that was just the way it was going to have to be.

"Well, then April said she was riding with this real nice guy."

"So April was hitching too?"

"I don't know if she was hitching or if she knew the guy. Anyway she said she was with him and he could prob'ly give us a lift."

"Where was he at this time?"

"Around."

"Around where?" Salazar had a lot more patience than I did. On the other hand he wasn't carrying around an extra person. And he hadn't spent sixteen years trying periodically to get some kind of sense into Hal.

"I don't know," Hal said. "Just around. Maybe he had to pee or something. I don't know. Just around somewhere. Then he came back."

"Came back from where?"

"I don't know. Came back from wherever he was."

"Was he on foot or in a car?"

"He had a car but right then he was on foot. I mean he was walking around somewhere."

"So he came back and then what?"

"So April told him about this guy—"

"This which guy?"

"The guy that grabbed Lorie. I guess Lorie must've told her while I was walking around. So the guy said he was a bastard. The other guy, I mean."

"The guy that was with April said the guy that tried to grab Lorie was a bastard," Salazar clarified. "That right?"

"Yeah, that's what I said. So the guy—"

"Which guy? The guy that was with April?"

"Yeah, that guy."

"What was his name?"

"I don't know. April kept calling him 'Sugar' but I don't think that was his name."

"Most likely not," I agreed.

"So the guy that was with April did what?" Salazar asked, after successfully wiping a smile off his face.

"He said he'd take us to this town that was on the main highway. He said he couldn't take us any farther but we could hitch a ride from there to Albuquerque real easy. So we went to his car.''

"What sort of car?''

"A Camaro. Red.''

"What year?''

"I didn't notice what year. It was pretty dark by then.''

"Okay, so now you and Lorie are in the car with the guy in the red Camaro. What does the guy look like?''

"Just a guy. Kind of ordinary.''

"Kind of ordinary how? Is he white? Black? Chicano? Indian? Oriental?''

"Oh. He's white.''

"What age?''

"I don't know. Maybe twenty or thirty.''

"Or twenty-five?''

"Maybe he's twenty-five. I don't know.''

"How tall? Is he closer to your height or closer to mine?''

"Kind of in between. And he wasn't fat or skinny. Just ordinary.''

From where I was sitting, I could see Salazar making notes. So far he had *W/M 20-30, 5'10''-6'2'', 160-180, med bld*. "Hair? Eyes?'' he asked now.

"Brown.''

"Both brown? Hair and eyes both?"

"Yeah. I think. Or maybe they were blue. And he didn't wear glasses."

Salazar wrote hair brn eyes unk. "How long was his hair?"

"Missionary haircut."

"Huh?"

"Mormon missionary," I clarified. "Post-boot-camp military. Right, Hal?"

"That's what I said." Hal sounded injured.

"That's what you thought you said."

"Okay," Salazar said, "how was he dressed?"

"Pants and a shirt and boots and a jacket."

"What kind of—'

"I was getting to that, Mom," Hal protested. "Okay. The pants were sort of grayish blackish."

"Charcoal?" Salazar asked.

"Yeah. Charcoal. And the shirt was blue. Light blue. And the boots, well, they were just boots. Plain boots. I mean they weren't cowboy boots. They were brown. And it was a sort of a nylon jacket, heavy kind of."

"Ski jacket?"

"I guess. I don't know what a ski jacket looks like."

"Fort Worth, no, I guess you wouldn't. What color was the jacket?"

"Blue. Navy blue."

"He have any mustache, beard, anything like that?"

"Uh-uh," Hal said.

So now we had a description of sorts. *W/M, 20-30, 5'10"-6'2", 160-180, med bld, brown hair military cut, eyes unk, LSW charcoal pants, navy blue nylon jacket, plain brown boots, driving a red Camaro, year unk.*

For what it was worth. Which might well be nothing.

"Okay, so he brought you here. Anything happen on the way?"

"Yeah, and I didn't like it."

"What happened?" Salazar asked.

"We stopped at a service station and when we got back in the car he made April get in the back with me and he made Lorie get in the front with him and I didn't like that."

"Did Lorie?"

"No. And neither did April. She was mad."

"Lorie was mad, or April was mad?"

"April was mad. I think Lorie was scared."

"Why was Lorie scared?"

"This guy just kept looking at her."

"Looking at her how?"

"You know how," Hal said, sounding for a moment as if he had halfway good sense. "The same way that other guy kept looking at her. I didn't want him to look at Lorie like that. I said maybe Lorie and I ought to get out and walk and he said why'd we want to do that, when we were almost there? And then he said he'd buy us supper and I said I'd buy us supper and he said, 'Kid, save your money,' and I didn't know what to say and anyway he wouldn't stop the car. So he said again he'd buy us supper and Lorie said okay. And then we got into this town."

"Which town?"

"This town. The one we're in."

"Las Vegas."

"Yeah, if you say so. And so we went to this restaurant and he bought us supper."

"What restaurant?"

"I don't remember."

Salazar started rattling off names. You wouldn't think a town the size of Las Vegas, New Mexico, would have more than about three restaurants, but by the time Salazar ran out of memory and pulled out the Yellow Pages I was beginning to think there were about as many restaurants here as in Fort Worth.

After Salazar's third trip through the phone book Hal settled on K-Bob's. He thought. He wasn't quite sure but he thought that sounded right. He had a salad there and it had this sort of pink goop on it and he had a hamburger steak and French fries and iced tea. He looked rather guilty about the iced tea and I ignored him. I don't care if he drinks tea. He's the one who decided to be a Mormon.

He was prepared to tell us what everybody had to eat, but Salazar didn't want him to. Then he reconsidered. "What did April have to eat?" Hal told us.

"And this was about what time?"

Hal dithered a little and finally settled on about nine-thirty. He didn't ask why Salazar wanted to know. I didn't either. But then I already knew that if the pathologist knew what she'd eaten, and what time she'd eaten, he could get a pretty good idea from the condition of the stomach contents about exactly what time she'd died. Which might, or might not, but most likely wouldn't, help Hal.

"So you ate and then what?"

"So he said he and April were going to a motel and he offered to get us a room and Lorie and I said no, we'd camp out. He said it was going to be cold and I said that was okay, we had warm sleeping bags. So then he tried to kid us and then he got kinda mad, but finally he said he'd take us to a place we could camp."

"So you were stupid enough to get back in the car with him," I said.

"Mom, he didn't do anything bad, he just looked at Lorie funny. That wasn't any reason to snub him. And he just took us to that square kind of place and let us out there and he and April drove off."

"Then what?" Salazar asked, forbearing to point out that if Hal hadn't killed April, then "the guy," whoever he might happen to be, most likely had.

"Then Lorie and I unrolled our sleeping bags and went to sleep. We were both some more kind of sleepy, and Lorie said it was that stuff she took for cramps, but I think it was just all the walking and everything, because I didn't take any medicine. So we both went to sleep. And then the next thing I knew I woke up in the middle of the night because I had to pee and I got up and sort of walked around to pee and then... and then..."

"And then what?"

"There were some lights. Not much, it was pretty dark, but there were some lights on the square. Enough for me to see something red and shiny in Lorie's sleeping bag. And I wondered what and I leaned over to see and then I saw... that girl. April. I saw her and... and, she was dead. I mean she had to be dead. And I stood up to see if Lorie was okay,

I mean, to find Lorie, and then there was this spotlight and this cop started yelling at me."

And the story, from there, we knew.

But we were no further at all on the important questions. The ones like, where was Lorie? And who was April? And how did April get in Lorie's sleeping bag?

And who killed April, and why did he do it with Harry's hunting knife?

"April didn't tell you anything at all about herself?" Salazar asked. "Her full name, where she came from, anything?"

"Not me she didn't," Hal stated positively. "If she told anybody it was Lorie. But she didn't tell me."

FOUR

"IS HE ALWAYS like that?" Salazar asked me.

"Like what? Scatty, you mean?"

Salazar thought about it. "Yeah," he said. "Scatty. That's a pretty good word."

"More or less," I said. "He's not stupid. He makes decent grades in school most of the time. It's just—well, the doctor says most likely it's mild brain damage, either at birth or just because his natural mother was severely malnourished. Officially it's severe hyperactivity."

"What age was he when you found out?"

"Three or so, why?"

"And by then it was too late to do anything about it?"

"Oh, sure, if it was prenatal or a birth injury, there's just nothing—"

"I mean the adoption. It was already final?"

"What does that have to do—" And then I stopped, realizing what Salazar was asking me. "Look," I said, "we adopted Hal when he was three months old. Kids aren't fish. You don't throw them back if they aren't just right."

"Some people do," Salazar muttered neatly squaring his clipboard on his neatly squared desk pad. He looked up at me, dark eyes unfathomable, and repeated, "Some people do."

I didn't know what to say to that, so I didn't say anything. Salazar flipped open the case file and handed it back to me. "Have a look," he said. "I'm going after coffee. Want some?"

"Uh-uh. Thanks."

"Get you anything? A Coke maybe?"

"A Diet Coke would be super. Thanks." I was sounding like Hal, inane, a broken record. But Salazar had sounded so bitter. Had he been adopted and then unadopted? Had somebody thrown him back like a fish that wasn't a keeper?

If so it was none of my business. I concentrated on the file folder, which not to my great surprise contained exactly nothing I didn't already know.

Salazar came back in with his hands full, coffee and two Cokes. "I'm taking one back to the kid," he said. "Those sedatives, they make your mouth pretty dry."

The kid, of course, was Hal, back in a locked holding cell again. He had protested about that, and I told him it was just for a little while, don't worry about it, and gave him a paperback mystery I had stuck in my purse for reading on the plane.

I hoped it was just for a little while. As Salazar had quite rightly pointed out after returning from locking Hal up, he certainly couldn't be released. Not yet. We had nobody's word but his for anything that had happened from the moment he left Fort Worth. No corroborating testimony, no physical evidence, no nothing.

I believed Hal was telling the truth. Salazar didn't say he didn't believe it, but he didn't say he did believe it, either. He couldn't. Not when Hal had been found leaning over the body with blood on his hands and blood on his clothes, with a knife he'd brought from home lying at his feet marked with blood and tissue.

"We don't have facilities here for juveniles," Salazar said, when I handed the folder back. "We don't normally keep juveniles here. We don't normally keep anybody here for long."

"You send 'em to Santa Fe?" I asked. That made sense. Santa Fe was the nearest town of any size, as well as the state capital.

But Salazar shook his head. "Adults, yes. But not juveniles. They go to Nevada."

"To Nevada?" That sounded peculiar to me.

"It's a multistate arrangement. It just doesn't make sense—Oh hell, you don't need to know that, why should I bother to explain?"

He was right. I didn't need to know that. Being from Texas, I wasn't much better equipped to understand the problems of small states than I was to understand the problems of small towns. Anyway I didn't want to know all about New Mexico's problems in dealing with juvenile offenders. All I wanted to know was "So what about Hal?"

"If it's okay with you—understanding that cell isn't really meant for long-range use, which means he's going to be in cramped quarters—I'll go on and keep him here for now. We might want to talk with him again. And—well, I just have to check out his story some before I make any kind of decision."

Rather encouraging. Salazar wasn't prepared to say he accepted Hal's version of events, but his hesitancy now hinted that he might be at least leaning toward accepting it.

So now I had to call Harry and let him know that Hal was still in jail, Lorie was still missing, and I wasn't likely to be heading for home very soon. I had to call Donna and let her know—what? That Lorie was still missing? That Lorie might well be in the hands of somebody who'd already killed at least one person?

I did not want to call Donna. But of course I had to.

Pending the arrival of the lab crew from Santa Fe, there didn't seem to be much for me to do. As it appeared that I was going to be in Las Vegas, New Mexico, for considerably longer than I had planned, I'd better use the available time to go get a motel room.

So I went and got a room—there were plenty of motels as well as plenty of restaurants—and I called Harry and told him what was going on. Harry reminded me I was supposed to be having a baby in about two weeks, and I agreed that I knew that, but right now I had to call Donna, 'Bye. Then I called Donna, but to my relief she was out and I just left a message on her answering machine that we were working on it and I'd call again when I had more news. I called Salazar and let him know where I was staying. And then I went out and hunted up a bookstore, but as the only bookstore I found was a very high-quality one dealing only in Western Americana, which was not what I was looking for, I wound up in the ubiquitous K-mart, which has invaded even the hinterlands of New Mexico. There I bought Hal a *Mad* magazine, a *Field and Stream*, a few paperbacks, and—with a certain small amount of malice—a pocket atlas. To make up for the atlas, which he would doubtless—and rightly—regard as an insult, I tried to find him a *Dragon* magazine, but there weren't any, so I got him a *Dungeons and Dragons* module. I wasn't sure what he'd do with it without a dragonmaster and a pocketful of those umpteen-sided dice the game seems to demand, but he had enough of the dice at home and I utterly draw the line at playing Dungeons and Dragons myself. Maybe he could just read the module or something. On second thought I added a package of graph paper. He could spend his time in the slammer drawing dungeons.

I dropped off the stuff for Hal—including some munchies; the kid normally eats about fourteen times a day—by the police station. The dispatcher said she'd get it to him, and told me Salazar had gone out to the scene with the lab crew. Seeing no reason to join them, I went back to the motel and tried to arrange myself into a halfway possible position for sleeping, out of which I was roused a while later—I don't know how long a while because I didn't look at my watch before I went to sleep—by somebody at the door. I opened it and Salazar came in and unceremoniously dropped a handful of black-and-white photographs onto the table.

"Do any of these look usable to you?" he demanded.

"Usable for what?" They were all photos of April, close-up face shots. The blood had been washed off, the facial wounds closed. But there was no getting around the fact that she still looked dead.

"Usable for newspapers, TV stations. We've got to get her identified some way. We've already run her prints through Santa Fe with no make."

I picked out a couple of pictures that seemed the least obviously corpselike and he said thanks, he'd get a batch of them printed up. He headed for the door again, turned, and added, "The afternoon shift at K-Bob's goes on at two-thirty. I couldn't get any sense out of Hal trying to find out where they stopped for gasoline—it could have been anywhere from Santa Fe to Taos to Mora—so there's no way of verifying that. Tomorrow morning I'm going to Bandelier. You want to go too?"

"Yes," I said. "And I want to go to K-Bob's too."

"Okay."

With that he was gone, and I got out my map to try to figure out where Bandelier was.

Nobody but Hal, I decided a few minutes later, could leave Los Alamos headed for Santa Fe on the way to Albuquerque and wind up in Bandelier National Monument. Santa Fe is south-southeast of Los Alamos. Albuquerque—if you want to go down the Rio Grande instead of down the highway, which takes you through Santa Fe—is south-southwest. Bandelier is almost exactly due south.

I went back out and got some lunch and looked over the town. There wasn't much to look at. A college (small), a library (smaller), a river that could be made into a tourist attraction but hasn't been, a lot of small stores that obviously do aim at tourist trade, a lot more assorted stores and small businesses that don't aim at tourists. It seemed that no matter where I went I kept winding up back at the square, where the crime scene crew from Santa Fe was still working. The crowd, for the most part, had gotten bored and left, and I had altogether too good a view of sleeping bags, backpacks, canteens, and so forth with which I was very well acquainted and which were now no longer good for anything except evidence. April had been removed; Harry's knife had been removed; everything else was still there.

At one-thirty I went back to the police station. Of course it was too early but I was antsy. Salazar let me come in to hear the lab crew explain that there were no usable fingerprints on anything. I would have been somewhat astonished if there had been. That stuff is stored year-round in the back of a pickup truck that does not live in a garage.

Salazar told me he'd had to figure out some official status for me, and he'd talked to the city attorney, and I was temporarily "on loan" from the city of Fort Worth (without the city of Fort Worth being consulted) and therefore I was—temporarily—a detective in Las Vegas.

That was nice, I guess. I prefer to have some sort of official status.

Salazar even lent me a badge and had somebody make me up an ID card. I now had two badges, except that I'd have to give this one back eventually.

And finally we went to K-Bob's. K-Bob's is a chain of restaurants—I remembered eating at the one in Wichita Falls when we were there for some sort of Elks convention—and, like most restaurants that are part of chains, this example was not exactly distinguishable from any other K-Bob's anywhere in the southwest.

Salazar had a copy of the photograph of April, and I had the photograph of Hal and Lorie at the Western dance, and after awhile a waitress—a big rawboned blonde with braids pinned on top of her head; she looked like someone who belonged in Minnesota rather than New Mexico—said with a slight but perceptible Spanish accent, "Oh, yeah, I saw them. Gosh, what happened to that girl? She looked a lot better last night. Is she sick or something?"

"She's dead," Salazar said flatly. "Now, these three were in here, right? Who else was with them?"

"Dead? Was she the girl in the plaza? I heard about that! Grace, Dolores, come'ere, remember these guys from last night? That's the girl that got murdered in the plaza! Who did it? Was it that big foreign guy? I'll bet it was that big foreign guy, wasn't it? That big one? This one right here?" She was, of course, pointing at Hal.

By now four waitresses were clustered around staring at the picture, and the few customers in the restaurant at this unpopular hour were gathering around, looking interested. Of this we make juries, I thought angrily, and said, "You sure do jump to a lot of conclusions fast, don't you? All Chief Salazar told you is that she's dead, not how or where or by whom."

She looked stunned, and into the silence Salazar said quickly, "Who was the other person with them? We know there was one, but what did he look like?"

There's no use recounting the fiddling bits of description dragged out with forceps; the four waitresses all together were about as bad witnesses as Hal was, but the description—such as it was—matched the one Hal gave.

So at least we had a little bit of corroboration now. Lorie did get to Las Vegas alive. There was another man with Hal and Lorie and April last night. He was older than Hal by maybe nine or ten years, he was about six feet tall, medium build, brown hair in a traditional-style men's haircut, blue eyes (maybe), charcoal pants, light blue shirt, brown leather boots, dark blue jacket.

Which description could fit thousands of men anywhere, and as vague as the witnesses were, there would be no use calling a police artist up from Santa Fe.

We went back to the car. Salazar started the engine, turned on the radio, and we heard a commotion. The dispatcher, whose closed-circuit TV sees the chief's office only rarely but the jail all the time, was calling for backups to the police station. Patrol cars were en route.

By the time Salazar and I got there the commotion was over.

A very young patrolman called Larry Begay—Navajo, I guessed from the name—was in Hal's jail cell.

Hal was not.

To say this situation did not exactly make my day—or Salazar's—or for that matter Begay's—would be the understatement of the century.

Killing Hal—the idea I'd had in mind when I began this expedition—was sounding like a better idea every minute, especially after we found out that Hal had not only relieved Begay of his keys but also had used said keys to depart in a City of Las Vegas patrol car, fully equipped with siren, bubblegum machine (all right, flashing red and blue lights), police radio, and—exactly what he needed, exactly what I want him to be in possession of—a shotgun.

Fully loaded including one in the chamber.

The dispatch room was small; with Salazar and me both crowded into it, especially in view of my present condition, the poor dispatcher hardly had room to breathe. Not that the breathing problem mattered to anyone but her, because Salazar, after sending his patrol cars back out on the streets, had taken over the radio.

"Hal, this is Chief Salazar," he was saying. "I've got your mom with me. Can you hear me?" Releasing the mike key, Salazar asked me, "Does he know how to use a radio?"

"He should; it's enough like a CB and he's used that often enough."

"Hal, can you hear me?" Salazar asked again.

This time a scratchy adolescent voice replied, "Yes, sir."

"You just did a pretty stupid thing," Salazar said. "Why did you do that?"

"I'm going to find Lorie."

"How? What are your plans?"

There was dead silence for a moment, before Hal replied, "I'm going to look for her."

"Where are you going to look for her?"

More silence. Salazar handed the mike to me. "Hal," I said, "there are right ways of going about these kind of things. We know how to look for Lorie. You don't. Breaking out of jail and stealing a car isn't the way to go at it. If you have any idea we haven't thought of, you come back here and tell us and I promise we'll check it out. I want to find Lorie just as much as you do. But right now you've got to come back."

"I can't, Mom. I've got to find Lorie. And right now I'm turning the radio off so I can think. You guys make too much noise."

And apparently he did just that, because we weren't about to raise him again. After three or four tries, we gave up, and Salazar told the cars on the street—I think there were two of them—what was going on, just in case anybody hadn't already guessed. Then he telephoned the San Miguel County Sheriff's Office with the same information, so they could release it statewide. To everyone he gave the same instructions: "Subject is not, repeat, not dangerous. Do not attempt to stop the car. Just let me know which way it's going."

Then he hung up the phone and turned to me, shaking with laughter. After a moment of astonishment, I recognized the gallows humor that so often results in angry telephone calls from outraged citizens to the chief's office: cops making rude jokes where people are dead. The laughing-to-keep-from-crying syndrome, the if-I-had-any-brains-I'd blow-'em-out feeling that allows black depression to masquerade and be dispelled as black humor.

After another moment Salazar recognized the feeling in himself and quit laughing, although laughter still lurked in those nearly black eyes that weren't, now, nearly so secretive as they'd seemed several hours earlier. "I'd have done the same thing," he said. "When I was sixteen, if I'd thought Maria was in danger, I'd have done the selfsame thing." Moving out so the dispatcher could get back into her corner, he added, "It'd be a helluva lot funnier if the girl wasn't really in trouble."

Back in his office, Salazar turned to me and asked, "Where's he going?"

"How in the world am I supposed to know that?" I demanded.

"Well, you ought to know his mental processes better than I do, anyway."

"Nobody knows Hal's mental processes," I informed Salazar. "Not even Hal." I thought a minute and amended that. "Especially not Hal."

But Hal has been around me virtually all his life, and I've been a cop almost the whole time. He can't help having learned this and that. "Bandelier," I said aloud.

"What?" Salazar asked.

"Bandelier. If Lorie's with—whoever—well, look at it this way. He was with April at Bandelier. He picked up Hal and Lorie there. For all anyone knows, maybe he picked up April there too. And maybe he's taken Lorie back to Bandelier to try to pick up somebody else. If I were Hal I'd be going to Bandelier." And then I remembered that Salazar and I had already decided to go to Bandelier, though not for the reasons Hal was going.

"He's not going to get there," Salazar said. I stared at him, more alarmed than puzzled, and he said, "Gasoline. How would you go about gassing up a stolen police car?" And then Salazar started to chuckle again. "But that's not all."

"What else?" I asked resignedly.

"That kid picked a lemon," Salazar told me. "I mean, he has picked a real lemon. There's a leak in the radiator, a small one. Not enough to matter much, around town. You just add water every so often. We were planning on putting it in the shop as soon as the car that's in there came out. But out on the road—well. The only question is, What'll he do first, run out of gasoline or blow up the radiator? So we just head to Bandelier. We'll find him between here and there.''

"On what road?"

"Huh?"

"What route is he taking to Bandelier? And is he even headed in the right direction? Look, you don't know this kid. He once started out for Arlington and wound up in Denton."

Salazar, not knowing northeast Texas, stared at me blankly.

I tried again. "You ever hear of Wrong-Way Corrigan? Compared to Hal, he was a homing pigeon."

"Wrong-Way Corrigan wasn't hunting his Maria—or his Lorie." Salazar stood up, jangling car keys. "I'm going to Bandelier. You want to go or not?"

Of course I wanted to go.

WE WENT BY the back roads because Salazar and I decided Hal would figure—wrongly, of course—that a stolen police car would be less conspicuous on a back road than on the highway.

We were right.

The patrol car was parked on the shoulder of a two-lane road just west of Mora. The hood was up, and all I could see of Hal as he industriously fiddled with wires was the seat of his jail coveralls and points south. I winced; last time I parked on a major highway with the hood up an eighteen-wheeler came by, and its air turbulence closed the hood flat, utterly demolishing that pole thingie (look, I am not a mechanic) that holds the hood open. If I'd had my head under the hood, the crash would probably have demolished me. But either there had been no eighteen-wheelers here, or this car was rather more solidly constructed than my late Lynx, which, come to think of it, never fully recovered from a shotgun blast into the radiator about seven months ago. Hal appeared to be intact, although he was so preoccupied he didn't even hear us approaching until Salazar asked, "You out of gas?"

Hal jumped violently, bumped his head on the hood, and used a rather interesting word. "Sorry, Mom," he said sheepishly, and returned to looking at Salazar.

"You out of gas?" Salazar repeated, his right hand resting very, very casually on his gun butt.

"I don't think so," Hal said, ostentatiously ignoring the location of Salazar's hand. "Not unless the gauge is broken."

"Then what's wrong?"

"I don't know. There's this little red light on the dash and I don't know what it means. The engine smelled funny and then the car quit running. I mean right in the middle of the road. It just sort of said clunk and stopped. I had to push it off the road."

"Good thing you've been eating your Cheerios," Salazar said, removing his hand from his gun butt. "Or is that Wheaties? Show me the little red light."

I watched as the two examined the little red light and then Salazar returned to the front of the car, followed by Hal. "This," Salazar told Hal just a little bit sarcastically, "is a radiator. You know what it does?"

"Sure I know what it does. I learned in driver's ed and anyway my dad told me. It keeps the engine cool."

"And did they teach you in driver's ed to steal police cars?"

"What?"

"Never mind. What is the radiator supposed to have in it?" Salazar removed the radiator cap and sniffed.

"Water and antifreeze, why?"

"You know what this one's got in it?"

"Water and antifreeze, I guess. Why?"

"No, my boy, this one's just real full, chock full to the brim, of air. Hot air." Salazar tossed the radiator cap in the air like a coin, caught it in his hand, flipped it over on his wrist. "Let this be a lesson to you. Next time you steal a car, be sure it hasn't got a bad radiator. That'll catch you every time."

"Better yet, don't steal a car again," I said.

"Your mom is such a spoilsport," Salazar said. "Right? Okay, kid, lock up the car, bring me the keys, and try not to be such a jackass again. You're damned lucky nobody blew you away for this one."

"Are you going to arrest me again?"

"I never unarrested you. Do you know anything about finding missing people?"

"No, but—"

"Do you want me to look for Lorie and that son-of-a-bitch that killed April, or do you want me to waste my time looking for a smart-ass kid like you?"

"Well, I—"

"Gimme the keys. You don't need them to lock up the car. We'll get somebody to come over here and drive it back later, provided it's drivable."

"I can drive it—"

"The hell you can drive it. I already told you you're a jackass. Get in the backseat."

Hal got in the backseat, slouched across it, and sulked nearly all the way to Bandelier. I loved it. At six foot five, 180 pounds, Hal was definitely bigger than his classmates. He had been bigger than Harry for two years, and never mind how long he'd been bigger than me. He is also bigger than most of his teachers. Furthermore he is—according to his teachers and principal—somewhat too big for his britches.

It took a five-foot-four, 120-pound small town police chief to cut him down to size. And as I said, I loved it.

Just before we reached Bandelier, Hal suddenly realized exactly what Salazar had said. He sat up straight. "You're looking for whoever killed April?"

"Yeah," Salazar said.

"Then you decided I didn't."

"Tentatively."

"How come?"

"'Cause you're too stupid."

I winced, and Hal looked hurt. Then he asked, "Then how come I'm still arrested?"

Salazar cut off the engine, opened the car door, stood up, and turned with one foot on the ground and one where the running board would be if cars still had running boards. He began counting on his fingers. "Runaway," he said.

"Yeah, but—"

"Shut up. Runaway. Vagrancy. Indecent exposure."

"What?"

"Peeing on the grass in the town square in full view of a cop. Assault on a police officer, whom you're dammed lucky you caught off guard, because Begay could take your head off real easy if he wanted to. Escape. Auto theft."

"Yeah, but—"

"Did you hear me say shut up? Auto theft. And being a general nuisance. If you can behave yourself adequately for a while I might—might—consider dropping some of the charges. Providing you didn't kill April."

"But I—"

"Shut up," Salazar said. "When I want to hear from you I'll tell you so."

"Can't I even talk to my mom?" Hal protested.

"Your mom's busy."

I have played good-cop, bad-cop before. I, of course, always have to play the good cop. I'd guess that Salazar, deceptively small and delicate looking, most often played good cop himself. But right now he was doing an outstandingly good job of playing bad cop. I'd have to watch for my cue to play good cop, because in this situation it would be too easy for good cop and mom to get confused with each other.

Much too easy. Maybe I'd better just stay quiet and let Salazar play both roles. Which I was quite sure he would do extremely adequately.

The trouble was that neither Salazar nor I could guess how much role-playing Hal needed. Obviously he needed enough of a scare that he wouldn't take off like this again, or steal a car again, but had he told us all he knew about this case? About April? About the man in the red Camaro? Was he—inadvertently or deliberately—holding out on us?

Salazar was standing in front of me, arms akimbo, two fingers of each hand tucked under his gunbelt, looking at the collection of stone buildings that make up the park center of Bandelier, which is mostly (I found out later) a small archaeological dig and a lot of unimproved wilderness camping area. Hal was behind me, presumably still sulking.

Salazar said, "Hal, where was April when you first saw her?"

Hal did not answer.

Salazar turned. So did I.

Hal was gone again.

FIVE

SALAZAR WAS, OBVIOUSLY, faster than I was. At a guess, I would also say he was angrier. He had sprinted past me before I had even managed to register the fact that the police car was still there.

Well, of course the police car was still there. Even Hal was not scatty enough—or frantic enough—to leave his eight-and-three-quarter-months-pregnant mother stranded in the middle of nowhere without a car. But where had he gone, and how, and of course why? This time?

All that added up to one good question. It was one to which I did not have an answer, and by now, I had another good question. Where in the world had *Salazar* gone?

There was a brown park service pickup truck nosed in at the far end of the parking lot, but there was not a ranger to be seen. There was a café—souvenir shop roughly to my right, but the sign on the door said CLOSED FOR THE SEASON. There was a glassed-in room roughly to my left where brochures and books apparently were sold—at least I could see a rack of books and brochures—but I could also see, quite clearly, a padlock on the door.

A large black-and-white bird made a noise vaguely like a rusty nail being pulled out of an old board, walked toward me with its head cocked sideways as if it had been hanged (now why did I have to think that?), screeched again, and then apparently decided I wasn't ripe yet. It flew away into the top of a pine tree, where it sat and stared at me disapprovingly, screeching periodically.

Sorry, bird.

Wherever Hal had gone—wherever Salazar had gone hunting Hal—neither one of them was making very much noise about it.

Look, Fort Worth is not exactly Tokyo or Los Angeles, but all the same it's a city. And my neighborhood—Summerfields—is an unincorporated area, but let us say that the developers made maximum use of the land. There are always people, maybe not in the same room or even in the same house, but there. Somewhere nearby. And there is always sound. A jet overhead. The heater or the air conditioner or the water heater or the refrigerator. Cars outside. Somebody's dog—very often mine; Pat is half pit bull and very talkative. Dammit, I was not used to being alone—totally, completely, utterly alone—and now I was alone, except for the wind in the pine trees and a creek running somewhere nearby and that awful screeching bird. I'd asked often enough for some peace and quiet but this was too blinkin' much of it. I didn't like it, I wanted it to go away.

Ridiculously, I found myself shivering.

Well, maybe that wasn't so ridiculous after all. Maybe I wasn't shivering because I was alone. Maybe I was just shivering because I was cold.

March in Fort Worth isn't quite summer. You've still got your Easter cold snap to reckon with; it's too early to put the winter clothes away and turn off the furnace. But most of the time it's shirtsleeve weather. I wasn't used to the weather I was finding here, any more than I was used to the solitude, and, like the solitude, I wasn't liking it.

The snow was gone from the sunny meadow areas. But under the trees there was still a lot of it, and when I began aimlessly walking, partly hunting Hal or Salazar or a ranger or anybody, partly looking for evidence (though I had no idea what I expected to find), and partly just trying to warm up, I found that the creek I'd been hearing still had ice on it here and there.

Ice melts at 33 degrees, and over running water it ought to melt faster.

But of course the creek was heavily shaded, especially now, with the sun low in the west casting long shadows everywhere.

By now I had walked far enough down the path that I could see the cliff dwellings Hal had rather incoherently tried to describe. If it were not so near sunset, and I were here on vacation, if I were not getting ready to have a baby, I would head over toward them. Of course I was curious. I am always curious. I don't think anybody ever becomes a cop who is not consumed with curiosity. But clearly this wasn't the right time for me to go tour the ruins. I wasn't up to the walk or the climb.

The Anasazi women made the walk and the climb, pregnant or not. They had to. Their homes were in front of me, a mile or more ahead and up the sheer wall of the sandstone cliffs. And their water was behind me. They had to carry the water up the cliff, a chore that couldn't have been eased much by the beauty of their famous pots.

What kind of crime rate did the Anasazi have? They were the ancestors of the Pueblo, and the Pueblo are a peaceful people. But still, a lot of warm bodies had been crammed into a maze of small dark rooms. I had no doubt there had been murder done here before now, whether or not it had been done here recently.

What kind of repair were those cliff dwellings in? Were any of them at all usable by modern standards? My thoughts were gradually creeping back into their accustomed track, their police mode. Could the man in the red Camaro have hidden there? Had he taken April there? Had he camped there with April, before he killed April, if he killed April?

Had he hidden Lorie there?

Did Hal think he might have hidden Lorie there?

I suspected that Hal did think that. But Hal hadn't had time to get there yet, walking; neither had Salazar. And neither one of them was in sight. So Hal wasn't on his way there and Salazar wasn't on his way there. They were somewhere else in the dense pine forest surrounding the sunny meadow that lay between the cliff dwellings and the creek, and I couldn't help worrying about what might be happening wherever they were. Hal had pushed his luck too far.

I had been walking and cogitating; now, suddenly, I found myself standing still. I couldn't have gone a step farther if I'd had to, not until I stopped and collected my feelings and tried to figure out what was going on, which wasn't easy as I hadn't the slightest idea. Every hair on my arms was standing straight up, and I wouldn't have sworn the hair on my head wasn't doing the same thing. I felt—

Have you ever stood just a little too close to a big, big dynamo?

Have you ever been out in a thunderstorm and had that prickly sensation that says lightning is getting ready to strike much too near you?

It was like that. Only different. Whatever was giving me the feeling was coming from somewhere ahead of me on the path, actually kind of to my left from where I was standing facing the distant cliff. I wasn't sure I wanted to know what it was, only I knew I was going to go and find out because I had to. Anything generating that much power...

Only first I pulled off my jacket and tried to slick down the hair on my forearms, which persisted in standing straight up, and then I gave up and hung the jacket over my right arm and began to run my fingers through my hair.

And then I yelped, quite involuntarily. No one was there, and then, with no intervening time at all that I could ever recall later, someone was there, looking a little apologetic, as small and slim and dark as Salazar in that brown deputy-sheriff style uniform the forest rangers wear when they aren't wearing Robin Hood green. "You okay, lady?" he asked.

"I guess." I was still trying to get that prickly feeling out of my hair. "I just feel so weird. You got a generator here or something?"

"No. But it takes some people like that. Me, I never could feel it, but I've seen people a lot more shook than you on account of it."

"On account of what?"

"The Great Kiva. Come on, I'll show you."

I followed him around a curve in the path to the brink of what had to be Hal's absolutely indescribably wonderful hole in the ground. A kiva—a circular hole in the ground used by Pueblo Indians and their ancestors for secret and presumably sacred ceremonies—is customarily roofed over. This one wasn't, not any more, and probably no ceremonies had been held in it for about 1,200 years. But I was quite certain that whatever had made it sacred hadn't gone away. I could feel a staggering power emanating from it.

Quite suddenly, just as suddenly as it had hit me, the feeling was gone. I was seeing something in the hole in the ground, in the snow and the slush and the mud, that didn't have anything to do with the Anasazi or whatever they had done there, and my mind was no longer on metaphysics.

What I was seeing was a red head scarf.

A red head scarf that was mine.

And simultaneously I became aware of a loud altercation behind me, a baritone voice expounding vividly on the general theme of "You young jackass" and not-very-secure tenor voice protesting, "I couldn't help it if they were cleaning the rest rooms! I had to pee!"

"You need a bladder transplant," Salazar yelled, "but before that you need a brain transplant! You could get your fool self blowed away for—"

"Hal," I interrupted loudly, "did you lend my red head scarf to Lorie?"

Dead silence. Utter. Even that obnoxious bird shut up, and the park ranger stared at me as if he were afraid I was about to go off the edge. Salazar didn't say anything; he just waited. I am told that Indians are very good at waiting. I need to emulate that virtue. For the moment, I managed to do so.

Predictably, Hal got tired of the silence first. "I thought it would be okay if—"

"Hal," I repeated, "did you lend my red head scarf to Lorie?"

"Well, I thought—"

"Hal, did you—"

"Yes!" he yelled.

By now I could hear Hal crashing through the undergrowth toward me. I could not hear Salazar, but when I turned to look he was right beside Hal. His silence was partly the difference between five-foot-four and six-foot-five, but it was more the difference between sixteen and forty-whatever, and even more the difference between thoroughly together and totally scatty.

Also Salazar was visibly angry. For which I did not blame him. With the possible exceptions of Hal's father, his scoutmaster, his wrestling coach, his brother-in-law (the future psychiatrist brother-in-law, not the attorney), and myself, no adult can be around Hal for long without becoming angry. How angry depends largely on how close the involvement with Hal might happen to be.

Salazar at the moment was somewhat more closely involved with Hal than any sane unrelated adult was likely to want to be.

By now Hal and Salazar had joined me on the brink of the kiva and were looking down. "Did she have it last night?" I asked Hal.

"What?"

"The scarf. Did Lorie have my scarf last night?"

"Oh. Yeah."

"You sure?"

"Yeah, positive. She had it last night. She was wearing it at the table."

Regardless of Hal's assurances, it was possible that the scarf had gotten into the kiva yesterday afternoon, when Hal was here with Lorie. But Hal had been completely certain Lorie had not gone past the rest room, and if she was cramping, I could well believe it. The kiva was at least a quarter of a mile from the rest room.

"It was not possible that the scarf was anybody else's. I had tried—and abandoned—an elaborate embroidery project during the winter. The scarf was embroidered not with a rainbow and an airplane, but with half a rainbow and a fourth of an airplane. I could see the embroidery from here. It was definitely my scarf.

I told Salazar that, and he nodded. He turned to look at Hal. He reached in his pocket. He looked at Hal again. "Hal," he said, in a tightly controlled voice, "can you for five minutes do as you're told? Exactly as you're told?"

"I always—"

Salazar interrupted the injured innocence. "Can you? And will you?"

"Yes, sir."

"Splendid. Then you will proceed to my car. Go directly to my car. Do not pass go. Do not collect two hundred dollars. Look in the trunk. You will find there a camera case and a black briefcase. You will get them out and set them beside the car. Holding the key in your hand so that you do not lock it in the trunk, close the trunk. Bring the camera case and the black briefcase and all their contents, as well as the key, directly to me. Do not dawdle on the way. Do not pause to examine the scenery. Do not even stop to pee. Is that quite clear?''

"Yes, sir.''

After Hal trotted off, apparently docilely, in the direction of the parking lot, the ranger said, "Mind telling me what's going on?''

Salazar told him. In colorful detail, and the ranger swore. "I've seen the Camaro,'' he said, "but not to notice. You know. Not to notice the driver or anything. I don't remember seeing either of the girls.''

"Were they camping here? The guy in the Camaro, I mean?'' Salazar asked.

There was a long silence. "I don't know,'' the ranger said finally. "Summer I'd know, but not necessarily this time of year. Officially they weren't. Officially anybody's got to sign in with us before camping, but we wouldn't necessarily notice if they didn't. I'd like to say we would, but I'm not really sure. Thing is, all we've got is rough camping—no fireplaces, no running water, no latrines, no nothing anywhere but right here. This part gets a lot of use in the summer. But this time of year? Man, it's cold as hell when the sun goes down. We lock up and go home. I mean, well, home's a trailer in the park—we're here—but it's not like we were patrolling all night. I can tell you nobody was building a fire, unless it was a mighty small fire inside the ruins so we wouldn't see the smoke or flames. But there's a lot of places to hide. There's a lot of places to hide a car.''

"And a lot of places to hide a body?''

"Just about as many places as you want to think of,'' the ranger said. He gestured toward the ruins. "There's bodies out there we ain't never found and there's bodies out there we ain't never gonna find. A lot of people lived and died here. A fresh body? Maybe. Eventually. By smell and buzzards collecting. But maybe not. Maybe not ever. Depends on how well it was hid.''

"Hell,'' Salazar said. "Hell and damnation.''

"Sorry. That's just the way it is.''

"I know it,'' Salazar said, and glanced at me.

"I know it too,'' I agreed. "That doesn't mean I have to like it.'' I looked toward the parking lot, hoping Hall wasn't in earshot.

He wasn't. He was trotting back obediently, laden down with the camera case, the black briefcase, and the car keys. He had the leather fob of the key case between his teeth, apparently to be sure he didn't drop the keys. "Wipe off the keys,'' Salazar said, "and give them to your mother.'' He glanced at me. "On second thought, don't give them to your mother. Just put them down over there on that log in the sun. I'll get them in a minute,'' he added. "I don't like spit," he muttered under his breath, getting the camera out of its case.

Standing on the brim of the kiva, he took several photographs. The camera was good; by adding a telephoto lens, he was able to get shots that would look like closeups when they were printed. Then he looked at the rickety wooden ladder leaning down into the kiva. He looked at Hal.

"I'll go down and get it," Hal offered eagerly.

"I'd love to take you up on that," Salazar said, "but it's my job." He looked at the ladder again, rather apprehensively, and added, "Oh hell. You can hold the top of the ladder. I don't want it to woggle. And if you go wandering off while I'm climbing I swear I will kill you. Is that clear?"

"Look, I can get it for you," the ranger offered. "I've got to go down there sometime today or tomorrow anyhow, to get out some rubbish. People are so damned filthy sometimes."

"You can go down with me," Salazar said. "But you can't go down instead of me. It's my job."

With Hal gripping the two gray peeled wood poles that protruded from the side of the kiva, Salazar—complete with camera slung around his neck, notebook and pen and tape measure in his hip pocket, and evidence bags tucked into his holster (his service revolver was now in my purse)—headed down the ladder. The ranger—his name had turned out to be Nelson, which was startlingly un-Hispanic and un-Indian for his face and build—waited uneasily for a while, brightening only when Salazar yelled, "Hey, Nelson! Come on down here!"

Hal was still industriously gripping the poles as Nelson descended. I watched from the brim, feeling very uneasy. I ought to be down there too. It was my case too (only of course it wasn't) and it was Lorie who was missing, and she was my responsibility (only of course she wasn't). But logic ruled the moment. Possibly—very possibly—I could get down that ladder. I was pretty sure I couldn't get back up it, and calling a helicopter to descend into a kiva to get me out didn't sound like a very good idea.

So I thought for a moment, until I thought of Fergie. The glamorous princess or duchess or whatever she is. When Fergie was pregnant she skiied. She rode horses. She did just about whatever she wanted to. (She was also somewhat more than fifteen years younger than me, but I didn't let myself think about that part of it.) And after all, what was a ladder? Merely a simplified staircase. And it wasn't very far down. Well. Not very very far.

I approached the ladder.

"Mom, I don't think you better do that," Hal said nervously.

I peered over the edge, looking directly down the ladder. How sturdy was it? I didn't weigh that much even now. More than I should—the doctor keeps telling me that—but not that much.

"Mom, I *really* don't think you better do that," Hal said.

Of course he was right.

Of course I went down the ladder anyway.

In this matter Salazar undoubtedly agreed with Hal, but he didn't notice I was coming until I already was down. Judging from his remark, he might have been taking lessons from my husband Harry. "You got down here, you get back up," was all he told me.

That was fair enough.

So now I got to see what they were looking at.

It looked to me as if my scarf had blown in accidentally, or maybe—just maybe—been dropped in on purpose. It was caught on some wood that had thrown or been tossed in, but there weren't any footprints leading to it, and as slushy as it was down here, footprints would show.

As indeed they did, along the edge of the kiva, and even a glance was enough to tell me I wasn't looking at the footprints of either of the men who were standing there now. The footprints were those of a man—a large man, wearing sneakers. Well, of course

I couldn't swear that a man had made the footprints, but whoever it was had feet a lot larger than
mine, and mine are somewhat larger than I'd like
them to be. The second set of footprints, besides the
sets that Nelson and Salazar and I were standing in,
were those of a woman, and this time I was sure, just
about a hundred percent sure. They were the footprints of a woman wearing high-heeled sandals. And
yes, I knew they were sandals, because at one point
she'd sunk so deep in thick mud I could make out the
marks of the straps.

Now, admittedly I had not seen Lorie since well
before she left Fort Worth, and in fact I had not even
thought to ask Hal what footwear she had on, but I
have not seen Lorie in sandals since sometime last
fall, and I have *never* seen Lorie in high-heeled sandals. She simply does not wear high heels.

On the other hand I had seen a pair of hight-heeled
sandals lying on the ground between Hal's sleeping
bag and Harry's. A pair of high-heeled multicolored sandals with drying mud on the soles and parts
of the straps.

"You got plaster of paris?" I asked Salazar.

He looked at me in a tone of voice I do not like to
be looked at in. "No, I haven't got plaster of paris,"
he answered.

With Nelson holding the measuring tape open to a foot, Salazar took several photographs with the camera pointing straight down. They would be enough for an ident. He took similar photographs of the sneaker tracks. No, we didn't have any sneakers to compare with the tracks yet. But we would.

We were going to have to find them, if I was ever going to manage to take Hal home.

With the shoe tracks photographed and the scarf gathered, the three of us began to search. I wasn't sure what any of us expected to find in such an idiotic location, but that is very often the case—you search without knowing what you expect to find, hoping that you'll find something that will provide some sort of information that will help to clear the case. This time we were lucky. We found something, though how much good it was going to do I hadn't the slightest idea. The tracks led to a place where a fireplace had been built into the wall, probably when the kiva was new. Under the fireplace was a ledge that had remained reasonably dry even with all the snow and rain and slush that had fallen during the winter, and on that ledge there was a double sleeping bag. Beside the sleeping bag was evidence of another kind, a used condom.

Now, I had to do a little bit of thinking about that. Because if this was where April and the man in the red Camaro had made their camp, and if he had planned from the start to kill her, why had he bothered to use a condom? Why worry about not making a girl pregnant if he was going to kill her anyway?

I asked that, and Salazar said, "Maybe he wasn't planning on killing her. Or maybe he didn't want to kill her yet and she insisted he use it. Or maybe he thought she had germs. Or maybe she was on her period and he was squeamish."

Salazar, himself rather squeamishly, collected the condom by nudging it with a twig that had been beside it onto the top of an index card. "Got it in one," he said, displaying the trophy to me. There was dried blood on the outside. He slid it into an evidence bag and began to write on the label.

I thought of the scene in the city square. "Squeamish?" I asked.

"Well," Salazar said, and didn't finish.

"I just want to know why here," Nelson said. "There's a lot of places more comfortable. There's a lot of places easier to get into and out of. So why here?"

I wanted to know that too. I really wanted to know that. And then, suddenly, I remembered the feeling of power I had encountered just before I saw the kiva, and I started to shake. I looked over at Nelson, and I could tell that he was thinking of it too. I didn't want to mention it to Salazar. I didn't know if he had ever felt it, or if he had ever heard of it, and I didn't want him to think me some kind of nut.

I looked over at him.

He wasn't going to think I was some kind of nut. He was standing, staring fixedly at some point in the kiva wall that didn't mean anything to me but clearly did to him, and the set look on his face said he was thinking of something that wouldn't mean anything at all to me but—like the wall of the kiva—clearly did to him.

"Salazar?" I asked. "You okay?"

"I'm okay."

"What kind of Indian are you?" I blurted out.

Without turning, without looking away from whatever it was he was looking at that was not there, he replied, "Is that the question you really want to ask?"

No, it wasn't. He was right. "Do you know how a kiva works? Is supposed to work?"

"Yes."

"Does that tell you anything about—about what happened here?"

"Maybe." He turned to look at me. "Maybe. But I don't know for sure. All I can tell you for sure is— oh hell. I can't tell you anything for sure because I don't know anything for sure. But, it was blasphemy. It was blasphemy. I don't care what religion you are, it was blasphemy. Can you get back out of here by yourself? I've got to go get a big evidence bag."

I stayed in the kiva long enough to help collect the sleeping bag, which might not have anything at all to do with the crime, and then I managed to get back out of the kiva by myself, although I'll admit that by the time I got out I was wishing heartily that I had never gone in.

By the time I emerged, Salazar and Nelson were in a tight conference—tight meaning that they had their heads together, far enough away that Hal wasn't hearing them—and I ordered Hal to stay put while I walked over and joined them. The question turned out to hinge on whether they should go over and search the ruins now or wait. Salazar was in favor of searching them now. Nelson was explaining how long it would take for four people, one of whom wasn't exactly up to climbing, to search the ruins.

Nelson won the argument by assuring Salazar he'd call the park service headquarters and have some extra rangers sent in from some other parks and they'd mount a full-scale search at sunup tomorrow morning. Which was about the earliest anybody was going to be able to do any real searching there anyway.

Salazar, Hal, and I returned to the Las Vegas police car, Hal serving as pack mule to carry the photographic equipment and so forth. Salazar carried the collected evidence himself.

I tried, once, to ask Salazar what he had been talking about. "What's supposed to happen in a kiva?" I asked.

He turned on me sharply. "Would you ask a Mormon what's supposed to happen in the temple?"

"No, but—"

"Then don't ask me what's supposed to happen in a kiva. I'm not going to tell you. All that you're allowed to know you can find out for yourself by going to some place like San Ildefonso Pueblo and watching the ceremonials; you can find out a hell of a lot more than you're supposed to know if you read the right ethnology books. But I'm not going to tell you. I'll tell you what's *not* supposed to happen in a kiva. Whatever happened in that one is not supposed to happen. And that's all you need to know. Now or ever."

"What if they ask you in court?"

"Then I'll go to jail for contempt of court."

He meant it.

I shut up and looked at the scenery, what little I could see of it. Daylight Savings Time wasn't in effect yet, and the sky was full dark by now.

He drove for about thirty minutes in silence so brooding that even Hal didn't dare interrupt, until finally he said, "Okay, I'm sorry. It wasn't your fault. It's just—we get these damned stupid *pahanas* who want to play Indian and they try to stick their noses into four and five thousand years' worth of tradition and learn it all overnight and they learn it all wrong and they twist it until it's something the people it belongs to don't even recognize. You wouldn't like it if people made things that are sacred to you into some kind of playground. Well, guess what, we don't like it either. That's why tourists can't take cameras into San Ildefonso anymore."

"Are you from San Ildefonso?" I asked.

He brooded some more. "Not exactly."

"But you've been there."

"I've been there. I'm . . . allowed there. I'm allowed there in a way that you wouldn't be. If that makes any kind of sense to you."

"Okay," I said. "It makes sense. And if it means anything to you—if it helps any for me to say it—I don't try to smuggle cameras into San Ildefonso and I also don't wear shorts when I'm touring cathedrals."

Salazar chuckled. "Glad you see the similarity. Most *pahanas* don't."

"What does *pahanas* mean?" Hal demanded.

"It's a bastard word. It's a Hopi word that I stuck an English plural ending onto."

"Okay, but what does it mean?"

"It means white people."

"Then I'm not a *pahana*."

"True."

"Then can I go to San Ilde—whatever it is?"

"Sure. Just like any other tourist."

"But I'm not a—"

"*Pahana*. Right. You're also not a Pueblo Indian. Sorry 'bout that." Salazar did not sound especially sorry. In fact, he started whistling as he drove.

Hal brooded a little bit, and then cheered up. "Hey, Chief Salazar," he said, "do you have to lock me back up?"

"Is that a dumb question or is that a dumb question?" Salazar replied.

"You know I didn't kill April."

Salazar thought about it. "Okay, right, I am now reasonably sure—not a hundred percent sure, but reasonably sure—that you didn't kill April."

"Then why do you still want to lock me up?"

"Do you want me to recite the charges again?"

"Yeah, but I was trying to find Lorie."

"Tell that to Begay, especially when he and somebody else have to come out here tomorrow with a mechanic to drive back the car you stole."

"Yeah, but I didn't mean to…" Hal's voice trailed off and he regarded Salazar glumly. "Okay, I guess I did mean to. But I had to find Lorie."

"Did you find Lorie?"

Even I considered that a rather unfair question, and Hal's voice was aggrieved as he replied, "No, but neither did you."

"I had to waste my time looking for you. Give me one good reason why I should let you out of jail."

"I can carry stuff for you."

"I have hands."

"I would've gone down that ladder only you wouldn't let me."

"It was my job. You wouldn't have known what to look for."

"I can talk to teenagers."

Salazar opened his mouth, shut it again, and then managed a quick glance over his shoulder. "What makes you think we have any teenagers to talk to in this car?"

"I'm a teenager. April was a teenager. Lorie is a teenager. Whoever that guy is, he likes teenagers."

"You do have a point there. There's just one problem."

"What's that?"

Salazar pulled the car over onto the side of the road, put it into park, and turned to look at Hal. "Son, you're Oriental. How many Oriental people do you think we have in Las Vegas?"

"I don't know. How many?"

"Just about none. Maybe ten at the most. What we have is a lot of Hispanics and a lot of Anglos."

"*Pahanas*," Hal interrupted. He is always proud of himself when he has an interesting new word.

"Anglos," Salazar said. "Hispanics are *Pahanas* too, unless they aren't."

"Huh?"

"About half of the Hispanics are like me, they're really Native Americans with Hispanic names, like me. So they're not *pahanas*. But if they're mainly Spanish background then they are *pahanas*. Now forget about *pahanas*, okay? There's one more little problem we've got in Las Vegas, and it concerns you a lot more than who is or is not a *pahana*."

"Which is?" I was the one who asked the question. I was curious, too, by now.

Salazar sighed and started the car again. Pulling back onto the road, he said, "I hate like hell to say it, but we've got one hell of a lot of racism. We've got a lot of Hispanics that don't like Anglos. We've got a lot of Anglos that don't like Hispanics. Now like everywhere else—I guess everywhere else—the racists are a pretty small minority. But you look at it this way. What do you think is going to happen if this big, tall, good-looking, Oriental dude comes in and starts asking questions about the chicks? Well, if you ask questions about the Hispanic chicks the Hispanic dudes are gonna get some more kind of pissed. And if you ask questions about the Anglo chicks the Anglo dudes are going to get some more kind of pissed. And Hal, if the Hispanic dudes and the Anglo dudes get pissed at each other in the first place they probably won't have a rumble because they know I'll drop on all 'em if they do, but if they do decide to rumble they've all got enough of a support system that probably nobody is going to get hurt very bad. But what kind of a backup have you got? What kind of a support system have you got?"

"I'm afraid he's probably right, Hal," I said.

"I get along with people real good," Hal said, in a very injured voice that this time was only about a fourth put on. "Mom can tell you so."

"Does he?" Salazar asked me.

"Actually, yes," I said. "With people his own age."

"Hal, I'm going to have to think about it," Salazar said. "I mean, be reasonable, even if you didn't kill April—and you're right, I don't believe you did—you've still done enough you could get put under the jail for about the next ten years, what with stealing a police car, escape, assaulting an officer, and so forth. I can see a lot of extenuating circumstances. But I'm really going to have to think about it before I let you walk. I'm locking you up tonight. But I will think about it. I promise you that much."

Hal wasn't very happy about it. Neither, to be frank, was I. But Salazar was right.

SIX

BY THE TIME I got into the police station the next morning, Salazar had apparently been there for at least an hour. He had Hal sitting on one side of his desk looking extremely guilty, as well he might when the opposite chair was occupied by a glowering young man about six years older than Hal, a chunky fellow taller than Salazar but considerably shorter than Hal, whose dark squarish face was decidedly disfigured by a purplish bruise on the left corner of his jaw. It did not take much imagination to suspect that maybe, just maybe, I was looking at Begay.

Begay was out of uniform, and Salazar's face was extremely expressive. He was up to mischief, and neither Hal nor Begay appreciated his humor. Begay was in midprotest.

"Sure I can convince somebody he's Navajo," Begay said, "provided whoever it is never saw a Navajo, but me, I *am* Navajo, so for me to do the convincing—"

"I didn't say—"

"You said convince 'em he's my cousin," Begay howled, so frustrated he was totally oblivious to the fact that he had just interrupted the chief of police.

"Does your cousin have to be Navajo?"

"I'm Navajo," Begay pointed out. "Born to the stinking Water Clan and born for the Monster Clan, if it matters to you." (Here Hal unfortunately giggled, and Begay looked more outraged than ever.) "So how'm I supposed to have a cousin—"

"Well," Salazar said, "your mother's sister could have married a Mexican."

"But she didn't."

"But she could have. You can pretend."

"Anyway I never saw a Mexican that big either."

"I have," Salazar said.

"So have I," I said, "but before you decide to try to pass Hal off as a Mexican you better take a look at his school record. He's flunked Spanish two years running."

"This is the silliest thing I've ever heard of," Begay continued to storm. "I mean, look, the guy's a Korean!"

"I am not a Korean," Hal protested. "I'm an American."

"So you're a Korean American."

"I'm not a Korean anything. I just have Korean genes and chromosomes."

"So what am I supposed to call you?" Begay demanded. "Saying Oriental is about as stupid as describing me and Salazar and Chief Nockahoma all as Indians. We don't look a bit alike. Neither do Chinese and Japanese and Koreans."

With no difficulty at all, I at once diagnosed Begay as a baseball fan. I could see his point, although I very much doubted that Chief Nockahoma, the mascot of the Atlanta Braves, was any kind of Indian at all.

"So what am I supposed to call you?" Begay demanded again, probably rhetorically.

But Hal took the question seriously. "You could just call me Hal."

Begay said, "Oh shit!" and Salazar laughed out loud.

"I guess that'll do for now," Salazar added. "Okay, Hal, we'll keep that in mind."

Hal, for a wonder, was silent. Salazar abandoned the air of joking. "All right, Begay, you're absolutely correct," he said. "I can't pass him off as a Mexican. But he's right too. He is somebody that could get out and ask questions and maybe get some answers us grownups—yes, that includes you too, Begay—couldn't ask, at least not and get answers to. Kids talk to kids."

"I don't need a bodyguard," Hal protested.

"No, just a guard," Salazar said. "Oh hell. Begay, you want to step outside for a minute?"

"I want to go to the locker room and get into uniform," Begay said. "I don't want to spend the day—"

"You'll spend the day doing as you're told, just like everybody else on this department. Outside a minute. I'm still thinking."

Begay, looking as sullen as Hal on his worst days, got up and very silently went out the door, slamming it very softly but with a vicious little click that made it quite clear to anybody who was listening that he had slammed the door and would have slammed it a lot harder if he had thought he could get away with it.

"Look, Hal," Salazar said, "you've been so wound up about Lorie—and I'm not blaming you for that—that you've lost hold of whatever common sense you might possess. And yesterday we were all too tired to make sense. But listen to me now, and your mom is going to back me up in what I'm saying. Hal, I cannot turn you loose. I just can't. No, I don't think you killed April, and I think the DA's office will back me up in not taking a warrant on that—though I can't swear to that, because until we've got somebody else for it we've got a solid enough case on you. And of course I'm not really going to make a case on you for peeing on the grass. If you'd kept your head yesterday I could turn you loose—tentatively—right now.''

"But—"

"Kid, would you stop interrupting for about three minutes and listen to me? Yesterday you slugged a police officer. That's a crime. You escaped from jail. That's a crime. You stole a police car. That's a crime.''

"I was only borrowing—"

"Don't give me that shit. You slugged a police officer and escaped from jail and stole a police car. Period. And kid, you're going to court on that.''

My stomach didn't feel so happy. But again, Salazar was right. Some things cannot be allowed to slide.

"I've got to go to court?'' Hal repeated. "You mean I can't go home even when we do find Lorie?''

"Oh, you'll go home,'' Salazar said. "But you'll be going home on probation.''

"Mom—'' Hal sounded as if he was about to cry.

"Hal, he's right,'' I said softly. "He can't just turn you loose, not on stuff like that.''

"I'm going to be in a lot of trouble at church,'' Hal protested.

"You're also going to be in a lot of trouble at home. It's not as if you didn't know better. You do.

And it's even worse when somebody who does know better misbehaves than when somebody misbehaves who doesn't know better. That's why cops hate crooked cops so much."

"But I'm not a cop."

"You're not a cop and you're not crooked," I agreed. "But your conduct has been reprehensible."

"What does that mean?"

"It means you've been making a jackass of yourself," Salazar said. "Look, I'm doing you a favor. I'm giving you a chance to help this investigation, and if you do a decent job of that I'll tell the juvenile court judge about it. But I cannot—cannot—turn you loose on the street without a guard. It's not for your protection. It's for my protection. Got it?"

"Yeah, I guess," Hal muttered, with an expression that said he didn't really get it at all.

"There's this old saying," Salazar said. "It goes this way—CYA. That means Cover Your Ass. It means if you take a chance try to do it in such a way that if somebody gets in trouble over it, it won't be you. Well, right now I'm trying to cover my ass. So you go out and ask questions with a guard, or you sit in that jail cell and play tiddlywinks. And it's up to you which. I've given you the options."

"I want to go," Hal said, "but if I have to have a guard does my guard have to be Begay?"

"'Fraid so,'' Salazar said.

"Why?"

There was a long silence before Salazar said, "Look at this from Begay's point of view. You got away from him yesterday. How do you think that made him feel?"

"But—"

"You've got an advantage over people like me and Begay and your mother and just about everybody. You're big. You're bigger than about ninety-five percent of the people on the street, and you've let it go to your head. Well, I've got something to tell you. Begay's tough. Begay's a hell of a lot tougher than you are. You didn't get away from Begay because you're bigger than Begay; you got away from Begay because he trusted you, because your mom's a cop and she's up here helping us out, and so he wasn't on guard around you the way he would have been on guard around anybody else. But let me tell you something. Begay will never trust you again, not unless you prove to him he should trust you. And you'll never get away from Begay again. You think being big makes you tough. You think being big makes you smart. Well, guess what. It doesn't. All being big makes you is big. And I'm going to give Begay a chance to prove that to you, if you make him do it."

"That's not fair," Hal protested, and I had to laugh at his tone.

"Go watch *Labyrinth* again when you get home," I advised him. "It may not be fair, but that's the way it is."

Salazar stepped to the door of his office and called Begay back in. "Begay, I don't care what kind of cover story you make up. Any story or no story. Hal can be just a guy you met at the bus stop if you want to. But for today, you and Hal wander around town and ask questions. Try to stay back and let Hal get into conversations; you sound too much like a cop. I'm giving you just one additional order to add to that. Don't let him out of your sight."

"I won't," Begay said grimly.

"You need some money?" Salazar asked.

"For what?" Hal asked.

"I don't know for what," Salazar said. "Where do teenagers get into conversations with other teenagers? For pinball machines? Video games? Whatever they are now? Hamburgers?"

I dug into my purse and handed Hal a ten-dollar bill and all the change I had. "This may be the only time in your life I will voluntarily give you money to feed the video games," I told him, "so you better enjoy it while it lasts."

"You got cash, Begay?" Salazar asked.

"Yes, sir. Some."

"Keep track of what you spend. You'll get it back."

"Yes, sir."

I have heard more cheerful "yes, sirs" and seen more cheerful faces than I saw as Hal and Begay went out the door.

"Do you think that was a good idea?" I asked, after the door shut behind them.

Salazar shrugged. "Probably not. I've had bad ideas before now. And I'm sure I'll have a lot more. But there's one good thing about him being with Begay that you don't know."

"Which is?"

"Navajos hate corpses. Navajos—in general, with exceptions—believe in ghosts. They call 'em *chindi*. You kill somebody, you're liable to have his *chindi* wrapped around your neck for the rest of your life. Which means if Hal pulls another stunt like the ones he pulled yesterday, Begay'll stop him, but Begay won't risk killing him unless there's not one other thing left to try. And, I've got people on this department I can't say that about. Some of 'em I inherited. Some of 'em I hired. Let's face it, you don't—anybody doesn't—have any business on any police department anywhere unless you're willing to kill." He looked at me challengingly.

"I killed a man," I said. "About seven months ago. I didn't like it. But I had to do it so I did it."

"Sorry," Salazar said. "I didn't mean to bring up—"

"It happened," I interrupted. "It happened. That's all. I don't—have any ghosts."

"Begay would."

HAL AND BEGAY REPORTED back to us, later, on what happened. Their tape recorded debriefings weren't as formal as one might have liked, but they were very, very detailed.

Out on the street, Hal turned to Begay. "Hey, I'm sorry," he said.

"Yeah," Begay answered, hands in his pockets and shoulders hunched against a harsh wind that was taking no note of spring.

"I mean I'm really sorry. I didn't mean to hit you."

"Shit you didn't mean to hit me. You can't hit somebody without meaning to."

"I mean I didn't exactly think about it."

"You sure didn't. And you can be real, real glad I wasn't armed."

"Hey, I meant to ask you about that. How come you weren't?"

"Would you have taken my pistol if I had been?"

"Of course not. I just wondered."

"You busted my jaw and took my car keys but you wouldn't take my pistol. Sure. I just really believe that. And I just really believe the moon is made of green cheese."

"I needed the car keys and I didn't need a pistol. I already apologized about your jaw. It isn't busted anyway."

"It felt yesterday like it was." Then Begay grinned. "Okay, you didn't bust my jaw. But dammit, man, you weren't supposed to swing on me like that. I figured you were in on a bum rap. And your mom a cop and all—man, I trusted you. And I don't trust so many people, especially not inside of a jail cell."

"Look, I really am sorry," Hal said miserably. "I mean I'm really really sorry."

"Okay, so you're really really sorry. What good is that s'posed to do me? Is it s'posed to make me stop feeling like a jackass for letting you get away? What good . . ."

Hal thought seriously about it. "It might keep you from getting killed sometime."

"How do you figure that?"

"You won't trust anybody else in the jail."

Begay burst out laughing. "You better believe that. Okay, you're right. Maybe you've taught me an important lesson. I'll try to be properly grateful but not today."

"I still want to know how come you weren't armed."

"Because it's against the rules to go into the lockup carrying your sidearm. You put it in a little lockbox outside the jail, and if you think I'm going to show you where the lockbox is or how to get into it then you got mushrooms for brains."

There's no need to trace their steps all over town. There are places kids go, there are places teenagers go, and Larry Begay was young enough to know where those places were even if he hadn't known from being a cop, as of course he had known. And twenty-one isn't that far off sixteen. By noon, while Salazar and I were still asking a lot of people a lot of questions and getting no answers at all, they were calling each other Hal and Larry, laughing over video games, and getting along just fine, although—as Salazar had warned—Begay still didn't trust Hal and made no bones about showing his lack of trust.

But how much Begay trusted Hal was about to stop mattering, at least so far as this investigation was concerned, because at an ice cream parlor on the square where they had stopped to get hamburgers Hal had just overheard the name April. He nudged Begay, and Begay nodded and reached in his pocket. He had his badge case out and in his hand by the time he arrived at the table where the four girls who were talking about April were sitting.

And by twelve-thirty, we were sitting in the muster room, because Salazar's office was too small for this many people. Hal, Begay, Salazar, and I had now been joined by Lydia Morris, Ione Aristides, Miranda Mendoza, Dawn McKay, and their teacher Teresa Butler. They were all from Armand Hammer's United World College, which to my surprise had a campus in Las Vegas located in and around a remodeled Victorian monstrosity of a building locally referred to as The Castle, and they had just identified April's photograph as being that of their good friend April Greene of Richmond. Not Richmond, Virginia, but a Richmond that is just outside of London, England.

The girls all spoke English with varying non-American accents, and despite casual dress they all had the unmistakable air of having far more money than was likely to be good for them. But right now they were thoroughly upset, most of all Teresa Butler, a slightly too-polished woman in her mid-thirties.

"Why didn't you tell me she was gone?" she demanded for the fifth time. "Why did you keep covering up for her?"

"We didn't want to spoil her holiday," Lydia Morris said, with an upper-class British accent.

"Holiday! Lydia, the child is dead!"

"But we didn't know she was going to be dead," Ione protested. "She was just—"

"Was just what?" Teresa Butler demanded. "She was just what?"

"Nothing," Ione muttered.

"She was going to have some fun," Dawn said. "She was tired of rules and rules and rules—"

"Rules! Child, you don't know—"

"Quit calling us children," Miranda said softly. "We aren't children and you always treat us like children and that's probably half the reason April left. She wanted to have some fun."

Salazar, who had been watching and listening intently, decided to interrupt. "How long ago did April leave?" he asked.

"I would rather like to know that myself," Teresa Butler said.

The girls looked at each other; some unspoken conference was evidently going on. Then Miranda, who seemed to speak less than the other girls but more to the point, said, "She's been coming and going. This time, about three days."

"You mean she's taken off before?" Butler demanded.

"She had a boyfriend," Dawn said.

"He was a real hunk," Lydia added, and giggled.

"A real hunk?" Salazar said. "Then you saw him?"

Again the girls looked at each other. "I didn't," Lydia said. There was a murmur of agreement from everyone except Ione, who sat guiltily silent.

"Then how'd you know he was a hunk?" I asked.

"That was what April said."

"Oh, April said he was a hunk? What about it, Ione?" So Salazar had not missed the one girl's silence; he was now staring at her, as hard and aggressively as he possibly could; with my eyes (less judgmentally, I hoped), Hal's eyes (extremely curious), and Begay's eyes (about as aggressive as Salazar's; in a culture in which staring is socially unacceptable it is impossible to stare politely) all on her, she wilted rather rapidly. "Yes, I saw him," she said, and burst into tears.

That necessitated a brief delay while she was comforted by her friends and, perfunctorily, by her teacher, before she decided to emerge from behind her handkerchief (lace) and look at me.

I don't know why me. Perhaps I looked the least threatening of the official and semiofficial faces clustered around.

"Can I talk to you alone?" she asked.

I looked at Salazar, and he shrugged. "What the he—heck. I'll let you use my office."

Which did not contain a typewriter, so if this girl, Ione, did happen to be prepared to make an official statement of any kind, I was not prepared to take it. Not that it mattered. She was not prepared to make a statement. She wanted to talk to me in absolute confidence that I wouldn't repeat what she had to say to Salazar or anybody else.

"I can't make that sort of a promise," I said.

"But why?"

"Ione, your friend is dead and we have to find out who killed her. Furthermore, there's an extreme likelihood that my son's girlfriend—and she's only fifteen—is now in the hands of the person who killed April. We want to get her back alive. This means that we have to make use of anything you tell us that can possibly be used. I can promise you that anything you tell me which does not appear to have a bearing on the investigation will not be repeated. But that's the best I can do."

Ione sat and fidgeted and dithered. She had a very pretty signet ring on her right ring finger, and she twisted it around her finger so many times I was beginning to be afraid she was going to wear a blister on her hand before she finally said, "I guess you have to know. The autopsy would tell you anyway. April is—April was going to have a baby.''

"Oh?"

"The other girls didn't know. She just told me."

"So I guess she was pretty upset."

"No."

"She wasn't upset?"

"No, because he wanted the baby." Ione twisted her ring some more. "She told me he was already married, but he and his wife didn't get along, and he had told her he was going to get rid of his wife and marry her—April—but he had a baby from that marriage and he wanted April to take care of that baby and her baby as well. He told her he loved kids. He wanted a whole lot of kids."

"So what did April think of that?"

Ione twisted her ring, and an expression of intense discomfort crossed her face. "April told me she'd promise anything, but it was a long way from promising to doing, and she wasn't going to take care of somebody else's brat. She said one of her own was bad enough and she wasn't even sure yet she was going to do that. I asked her what she meant, and she said she might get rid of it. I told her that's a sin, and she just laughed and said she didn't believe in sin. How can you not believe in sin?"

"Who knows? Go on."

"Go on how? That's all. She just told me that. I think she was drunk."

"Did she get drunk very often?"

"Pretty often, yes."

"Now tell me about her boyfriend. What was his name?"

"I don't know. I never met him."

"You said you met her boyfriend."

"No, I didn't say I met him."

"But you said—"

"I said I saw him. I never said I met him. She was very mysterious about him. She didn't want any of us to meet him. But one day I saw her downtown and he was with her."

"How did you know that was her boyfriend, if you never met her boyfriend?"

Ione grimaced. "It was quite obvious," she said primly.

"But April didn't introduce him?"

"April pretended she didn't see me."

"So you don't know his name."

"No. April always called him 'Sugar.'"

Hal had told us the same thing. And we weren't exactly going to put "Sugar" on NCIC no matter how many women he had—or might have—murdered.

"Can you describe him?" I asked.

She launched into a description that, roughly, except for clothes, matched the previous descriptions. That was good enough. "Let me go talk to Salazar," I said. Without waiting for Ione's consent, I stepped to the door and called Salazar into his own office, to give him what little Ione had given me, as Ione sat hunched over and fiddled with her ring.

Then he turned to Ione. "If we had a fellow come up to work with you, do you think you could come up with a recognizable—"

"Oh, I can't draw!"

"You don't have to draw."

"And those drawing things, what do you call them, Identikit, they never made sense to me. I don't see how you could even recognize yourself—"

"This one isn't drawing at all," Salazar said patiently. "It's sort of a photographic montage."

"Really? I never heard of such a thing. It's not Identikit? I read about Identikit in a book, but—"

"This isn't Identikit, but it's kind of like Identikit. I think what we'd better do—"

WE HAD IONE ARISTIDES, three waitresses from K-Bob's, and Hal all working with the Santa Fe identification technician, who came up with the photographic montage kit in a dark blue Sirchie case. Salazar and I watched; Begay—to his own obvious relief—had been turned loose to don his uniform and go back to looking like a policeman.

With that many witnesses—well. Any person who's been a police officer more than about three weeks is likely to be very highly aware of the severe limitations of eyewitness testimony. Personally, I wouldn't hang a dog on eyewitness testimony alone; I'd have to have some of that despised-by-the-layman circumstantial evidence to go with it. No two people—ever—see any incident, any person, exactly the same way; in fact, it is practically an axiom that if you ever do get two people who agree absolutely on the details of anything one or the other—and most likely both—are lying.

With five witnesses, we got a lot of contradiction, and the ident tech was sweating and pushing his hair out of his eyes a lot before an image was finally produced that all the witnesses agreed looked sort of like the man in the red Camaro (which Ione also had seen). All five of the witnesses agreed the composite could be made to look more like the suspect, but in view of the fact that they disagreed in different directions the only thing to do was to leave it as it was. At least for now.

The technician took several Polaroid photos of the composite and left them for us. The composite itself he took with him, to photograph again in the laboratory and turn the photos over to the news media, so that—we hoped—some member of the citizenry would see the photo and call us, or call the crime lab in Santa Fe to say, "Hey, that picture, you know that picture? It looks just like . . ."

And then we would check out the telephone calls, and nine times out of ten it would turn out not to be the right person, but then there was always the chance for that tenth time when it would be right. When somebody would go to knock on the door and see the red Camaro sitting in the driveway, and back off and wait for backup units, and maybe—maybe— maybe—get Lorie back alive.

There was one more unpleasant little chore remaining, after the ident tech left for Santa Fe and the four girls were dispatched back to The Castle—excuse me, to the United World College—in a police car. That was a formal identification of the body, and Teresa Butler seemed to be elected for that task.

April didn't look nearly so bad as she had looked this morning, despite the autopsy, because the skin was pulled back over the skull so neatly that unless you'd seen an autopsy you couldn't begin to guess how it had been pulled away. The openings in the torso were neatly stitched and covered with a sheet anyway, and the face had been washed clean. She was clearly dead; you would not look at her and think she was asleep, with the body now stiff and cold and the eyes in a permanent half-open position. But the raw horror of the bloody mess in the sleeping bag was no longer to be seen.

She didn't look so bad to me.

But I am used to the sight—and the smell—of corpses. To me the smell was there, of course, but even in my pregnant condition it had no particular effect on me. It had totally slipped my mind how it might seem to a person who had never before been in even the smallest of morgues.

Teresa Butler was not used to corpses. Teresa Butler was not used to morgues. She identified April and then started vomiting.

After she had recovered, she was asked to look over the things found on and with the body, to see if they were familiar. She identified the jewelry, the watch; she was calmer now. But then she came to the blood-marked leather ankle bracelet. She turned it over in her hand, gingerly, fastidiously; she wanted to help, but she didn't want to touch anything that had touched a corpse. She looked at me. "I never saw this before."

"But the rest of the stuff is hers?" Salazar said.

"The rest of the stuff, as you call it, is hers. But this isn't. Or at least if it is I never saw it before."

Salazar picked up the circle of woven leather, and looked at me. "We shouldn't have sent those girls home yet," he said.

"I can take you out to the school," Butler offered, looking at me. That was puzzling me. Even when she was answering Salazar she was looking at me.

"Go ahead," Salazar said. "I'll have Begay follow you out, to bring you back in."

"I'VE SEEN IT BEFORE," Miranda said. "Well, maybe not that exact one, but—"

"You mean she had several?" Teresa Butler interrupted.

Miranda looked at her. "She did not have several. To the best of my knowledge she did not have any. But they are made in my country. Poor people make them to sell in the markets."

"And what is your country?" I asked.

Miranda tossed her hair. "Yucatan. I live in Yucatan. My home is in Mérida. I am descended from the first colonial governor."

I was under the distinct impression that the first colonial governor of Mérida, along with all his family, was slaughtered by an uprising of Mayans who were not as subdued as he thought they were, but perhaps I was mistaken. At any rate I decided not to say anything. "So you think this may have been made in Mexico?"

"Yucatan. It may have been made in Yucatan. But it may not."

As determined as Miranda was not to allow me to call Yucatan Mexico, despite the fact that Yucatan definitely is a part of Mexico, I was beginning to wonder whether there was some Yucatecan separatist movement I'd never heard of. I gave up. Still looking at the bracelet, I said, "And you never saw April with it?"

"Never." Miranda tossed the braided leather back onto the folded paper I'd taken it out of. "It was a tawdry thing. Why should she want it?"

"But she was wearing it when she died. She must have wanted it."

"Or else that evil man wanted her to wear it. That is not impossible."

That was not impossible. It also was not impossible that Miranda was overdramatizing everything; she impressed me as being somewhat stagestruck.

I thought, not for the first time, that sticking a lot of spoiled rich kids in a remote place where they could not find anything to tickle their possibly jaded appetites and then, in the name of democracy, giving scholarships to a lot of poor kids and putting them in the company with the rich kids—who were bound, no matter how good their intentions, to make them feel left out—probably wasn't such a good idea. But then it was none of my business.

I put the leather band back into the fold of paper, replaced it in its evidence bag, and went out the door to where I could see Larry Begay patiently waiting for me behind the wheel of a marked police car.

"Glad you're here," he told me. "Salazar wants us both back ASAP."

"I hope Hal hasn't done something else," was my first thought, and I said it aloud.

Begay laughed. "Hal will stay out of trouble for a while. We had a little talk."

"His father and I often have little talks with him. They rarely do any good."

Begay laughed again. "How far will you go to enforce your little talks?"

"Well . . ." I said, and Begay said, "Exactly. I am considerably smaller than Hal. But he is afraid of me. Now." His cheerful grin rather belied the deliberately assumed Boris Karloff menace of his voice, and he failed to explain how this miracle had come to pass. I decided not to ask. At any rate Hal had no visible bruises, and gave no evidence of disliking Begay. So if Begay had successfully knocked some sense into Hal's head, far be it from me to ask how.

"The reason I called you in," Salazar said, "is because they put the composite on a news break and we're already getting people who think they recognize the picture. Deb, I'm putting you on that. Plan on hitting it first thing in the morning."

For a moment—just a moment—I felt offended. Who gave him the right to give me orders? All I had done was offer to help out.

And then I quit being offended. Yes, I had offered to help out. And he had taken me at my word and issued me a badge and an ID card and was treating me as a member of his department, and I certainly had no right at all to complain about that. If I didn't like it, all I had to do was say I'd changed my mind about feeling like working.

And then I could go spend the rest of the time until all this was over sitting in my motel room worrying about Hal and Lorie.

I took the list of names and addresses, looked at it, asked for a city map (which Salazar handed me at once; he must have anticipated the question), said, "I don't know how long it will take me to get to all these," and departed.

Leaving Hal still—or again, or however you want to put it—in jail.

SEVEN

I WAS USING MY rented car, and it occurred to me to
wonder whether Avis might not void my insurance if
they knew I was using the car to do police work. But
I decided not to let that bother me. Instead, I sat in
the car after breakfast and tried to collect my
thoughts.

On the seat beside me was a police walkie-talkie;
Salazar had told the dispatchers I might be on the air
sometimes. It wasn't, he'd commented, quite safe for
me to be running around without one. "Besides,"
he'd added, "I get tired of having to try to find you
by phone or go look for you if I need to ask you
something."

I could understand that.

I had the photograph of April, the one we'd decided was the best; an enlargement somebody had
made of a photograph of my photograph of the
Western dance, cut to show only Lorie's face; and the
photograph of the composite of the suspect, whom
I refused to refer to as "Sugar" no matter what April
might have called him. I didn't believe his name was

really Sugar, and I don't like to get all that familiar with criminals.

Not that we had any proof—yet—that he was a criminal. But we certainly had every reason to assume.

I also had an assortment of other photographs, male and female, of assorted age, races, and formality of pose, so that I could set up an impromptu photo lineup if I needed to, which I probably would.

I looked again at the list of names and addresses Salazar had given me. The Wardance Motel was on top. Somebody at the Wardance Motel—a woman by the name of Julia Gonzales—thought she had recognized the composite photo. Okay, the Wardance Motel it was. I checked the address and checked my map.

A motel could be a darned good place to start this phase of the investigation. Because motel customers fill out registration cards, and on that registration card they write their names and their home addresses and their car license plate numbers.

At least theoretically they provide such things.

The Wardance was an economy motel, and not at all ashamed to be viewed as such. It did not have a swimming pool; it did not have a restaurant; and, it developed, it did not have telephones in the rooms. What it did have was large clean rooms where people could sleep or watch TV. It's proprietor either did not want, or could not afford, telephones for the rooms. Besides that, if you don't have telephones nobody can steal the telephones.

It was the owner, or rather the co-owner, who had called. Julia Gonzales was a little Hispanic woman, much shorter than me, and probably about ten years younger. She had seen the composite on a news break on a Santa Fe television station, and she was sure she recognized it.

"Tell me about him," I said.

"Well, he comes over ever' so often," she said. "Not any special schedule. Just sometimes he comes here. He was here a couple of nights ago."

"Alone?"

"No, he had this girl with him. He usually does."

"The same one?"

She turned abruptly to shut off the small television that was blaring in the kitchen-living room-cum-office behind the registration desk, and then turned back to me. "Not always. But usually. For the last couple of months anyway."

I hauled out pictures, and she picked out April instantly. So it had been our unknown man who had stayed here, and I felt considerably heartened. We might be closing in on him.

He had given his name as Darren Fletcher, he had given a street address without showing a town, and he had provided a license plate number without showing a state.

Julia Gonzales couldn't tell me anything else. He'd never made a telephone call from the motel office, but there were plenty of pay telephones around and there was no reason why he should use the motel office for private business.

The room had been cleaned and reused since he had used it. Of course we could get somebody out to dust the room for prints anyway, but the idea didn't seem very practical to me, and I suspected Salazar would agree.

I radioed that I was going in and wanted to meet with Salazar, and the dispatcher radioed back that Salazar would be waiting for me.

For all the good it didn't do. Darren Fletcher might or might not be anybody's real name—somewhere in the world there must be a Darren Fletcher—but it almost certainly was not the real name of the man in the red Camaro. The street address did not exist in Las Vegas, nor—Salazar checked—did it exist in Santa Fe. Salazar said he didn't guess he wanted to check every city in New Mexico and I agreed; more likely the address had come out of somebody's head. And the registration?

Julia Gonzales had not, of course, gone out to look at the red Camaro herself, though she had told me the man was driving a red car and it might be a Camaro but she didn't know anything about cars. But like almost every motel operator, she had trusted the customer—the guest, as she put it—to know his own license plate number.

Which he quite possibly did. But this wasn't it. It didn't take long for the state computer to inform us that this registration was nonexistent, at least in New Mexico.

"Hell," Salazar said. That seemed to be his favorite word.

He sat and brooded for about forty-five seconds and then said, "Well, we couldn't expect it to be that easy. We've got Hal set for juvenile court tomorrow afternoon."

"What?" I said. That seemed to be quite a non sequitur.

"Look, you didn't come here to solve my homicides. You came here to take your son home. There's enough now nobody's gonna hassle me to charge him with the murder, and we'll get him probation for the other stuff. You might as well get on home. There's no sense—"

"Salazar," I interrupted, "I came here to take my son and his girlfriend home. Until we find Lorie I'm not going anywhere."

"Oh. Yeah." He brooded some more and I took off my jacket. It was getting warm in his office.

He abruptly sat up from the sprawl he assumed when brooding and stared at me. "A shoulder holster?"

"I certainly can't wear a hip holster now," I pointed out, and he chuckled.

"But a *shoulder holster*? I never saw a—"

"Salazar, I always use a shoulder holster," I told him, feeling unaccountably weary.

"Yeah? I mean, the only policewomen we have here are in uniform, so—but I thought—I mean, on TV women detectives carry their guns in their purses. At least I guess they do. I don't watch very much TV."

And like all men, I thought but did not say, you do a lot of generalizing. "Salazar," I asked, "you know how easy it is to take a purse away from somebody?"

"That makes sense," he admitted. "So somebody took your purse away from you one time?"

"Uh-uh. No, one time we were hunting a holdup man. It was late at night and it was chilly but my car heater was working a little too well and it was jammed open so I couldn't cut it off. So, as I said, it was late at night and we were hunting a holdup man. I didn't want to have to take the time to get my pistol out of my purse if I found him—I was riding alone. So I took it out of my purse and stuck it in my jacket pocket. And then it got hotter and hotter in the car and I took the jacket off and put it on the seat beside me. And by the time I spotted what looked like the car—half an hour later—I'd forgotten all about it. I thought my pistol was still in my purse where it usually was. And I grabbed my purse and got out of the car and pulled my purse open while I walked toward the guy I'd pulled over, and then I reached for the holster in the back of the purse and the holster was empty."

"Shit," Salazar said, making the word long and drawn out. "So then what?"

"So then I bluffed like crazy. Fortunately it wasn't the right car. If it had been, the bluff might not have done any good. So I let the man go and then I threw up. I was that shook up."

"I can imagine."

"And by then it was midnight. It was time for me to go off duty. And by the time I went on duty the next afternoon I was wearing a shoulder holster and I've used one ever since."

"Well, it makes sense. I just never thought of a woman wearing a shoulder holster. I thought—" He stopped to think. "I don't guess I thought about it at all. But if I had thought about it I would have figured your breast would get in the way."

Not a man to mince words, Salazar, or to be embarrassed by basic biological facts.

"Why should it? The straps go across your shoulders and back and the holster is in your armpit."

"I guess. I never wore one."

"Try it sometime. They're comfortable."

So comfortable, in fact, that a few times I had forgotten and had taken my jacket, vest, or shirt-jacket off, and had gone blithely off across the street in downtown Fort Worth in a blouse and shoulder holster. This always drew a lot of stares. I had no reason to tell Salazar that; he'd find it out himself if he ever started wearing a shoulder holster, and anyway, people don't stare as much at a man wearing a holster as they do at a woman. Even if it's a shoulder holster, which is really the only practical kind of holster for a woman to wear. Even if men don't think so. I mean, think about it. Our waists—generally, when we are not pregnant—are a lot more indented than men's waists are. This means that a hip holster, which lies reasonably flat on a man, sits at a very odd angle on a woman's hip, especially if she is what men call shapely. This makes the pistol harder to get at and harder to draw.

No, I'd definitely never, under any circumstances, even unpregnant, go back to either an inconvenient hip holster or an unsafe purse holster, although I do keep a pistol in my purse when I'm not on duty and not likely to find myself suddenly on duty.

Which actually can happen almost any time. There was the time this guy I knew was sitting peacefully in his car, reading outside a shopping center while his wife was buying a few groceries, and suddenly two heavily armed bank robbers burst out of a bank in the shopping center. That might not have been too bad except for several things: they recognized him, and he was in his personal car without a radio or even a CB, and he was not armed.

He didn't get a scratch, but I doubt his insurance company was too happy about the thirty-six bullet holes in his car. Not any happier than he was about having to, as he put it, just sit there and wave them good-bye.

I was mentally wandering, and Salazar was brooding again.

"What is it?" I asked.

He roused himself. "Huh?"

"Why the brown study?"

He shrugged. "I guess I'm worrying about what we *don't* have to go on."

"Meaning?"

"Look at it. An ankle bracelet that *might* have come from Yucatan, only there's no reason why it should. None of her friends ever saw it on her, but she hadn't time to go to Yucatan and get it, not between the time she went missing and the time she turned up dead. Your scarf Lorie was using, up there in that kiva. There doesn't *seem* to be any way it could have got up there unless Lorie went back up there after April was dead, but... but. We don't know. It's like—oh, hell. We've got a few fiddling little pieces but it doesn't even look like they're pieces of the same puzzle. And your Darren Fletcher. Okay, so there's no Darren Fletcher living in Las Vegas—and if he did why would he need to use a motel here?—or in Santa Fe or Albuquerque, at least not so far as I can tell from phone books, and he's not on NCIC, and that isn't a New Mexico license tag. But why shouldn't he live in Texas or Arizona or California, and why should he be on NCIC? I mean, unless he's killed more people than April, he started staying at that motel a long time before he committed—or probably even contemplated—murder. So why shouldn't he be Darren Fletcher? It makes more sense that he is than that he isn't."

"So you're putting him on NCIC with what we've got?"

"Yeah."

"You hear anything from Bandelier?" Presumably rangers had been searching that area since daybreak.

"Yeah. They found a fireplace where somebody had been camping in the ruins. Fire cold, nothing left behind. I mean nothing. So maybe it was Fletcher and April and maybe it was Fletcher and Lorie, and maybe it was some good camper who knew to pack all his rubbish out. Oh, hell!" He ran his fingers through his thick black hair, leaving it as tufted as a long shag rug.

"Oh, hell," he said again, and resumed brooding.

I interrupted again. "Any more calls come in?"

"Huh?" he said, sitting up straighter and blinking.

"Any more calls. People who think they recognize the composite."

"Oh. Yeah. Two or three dozen. You know how that goes."

Alas, I know how that goes. Put a composite—or even a photograph—on the television and everybody in the world has seen him. Well, it's not just that. Think about how many people swear they have seen Elvis Presley lately, when Elvis Presley is definitely and positively dead and buried, and you've got some kind of idea what police get when they're trying to enlist public aid in locating somebody. And unlike the *National Enquirer*, which can check out only the Elvis stories it thinks sound likely (likely to sell papers, that is), we have to check out every one.

So Salazar and I spread out a lot of index cards of names and addresses and telephone numbers on the desk, to try to rule out or at least postpone until later the ones least likely to be accurate and/or least likely to be useful, to try to decide where I should go and who I should talk with next.

After all, while the man in the red Camaro *might* have been eating a hamburger at Dairy Queen, what good did it do us, unless—and this was very unlikely—somebody at the Dairy Queen had gotten his license number? Or even knew him in person, which was even more unlikely, because if you know somebody in person you don't call the police and say "I served him a hamburger and chocolate shake at Dairy Queen yesterday." No, you call the police station and say, "Hey, you know that picture? It sure does look like..."

Or more likely, you call your friend and say, "Hey, this is funny, have you noticed how much that picture on TV looks like you?"

And then, if you're lucky, your friend laughs with you. And if you're less lucky your friend kind of grunts and then gets out of town fast. Or, if you're real, real unlucky, your friend blows you away before you have time to tell the cops.

So the man in the red Camaro might, or might not, have bought books in a nice bookstore on the square, the one I hadn't gone into earlier because it specialized in Western Americana and I was hunting Dungeons and Dragons for Hal. It was a crowded but meticulously neat place, two small rooms incredibly full of books, mostly of the very expensive coffee table or scholarly varieties and mostly so far out of my price range it wouldn't be worth asking the cost even if I did want them. There was a smattering of touristy stuff, again mostly informational. The man at the cash register—apparently the owner; I guessed he had retired from some other job and set out to make his previous hobby into a business or at least into a tax shelter—was friendly and affable. He didn't tiresomely insist that he knew the man in the photograph whether we believed him or not, but he did tell us he thought he might have seen him.

Where?

Well, walking on the square yesterday morning. Walking around looking at where all the police were.

It is certainly a fallacy, and it turns up now only in very bad mystery novels, that the criminal always returns to the scene of the crime. He certainly does not always; in fact, he usually doesn't. But every now and then he does. So it was not impossible that the man in the red Camaro had been walking on the square watching the police work.

And it became even more likely when the old man added, "He parked his car right in front out here," and gestured to the parking place I was now occupying.

"What kind of car was it?"

"Red Camaro." He told me the year.

"Did he have a girl with him?"

"Didn't have anybody with him."

"Damn," I said.

The old man—he'd told me his name was Rex Lewis—looked shocked, offended, and displeased. Apparently he does not believe women ought to swear. Or maybe he believes nobody ought to swear; I hadn't heard him swear himself.

"I don't suppose you got the licence number?"

Lewis looked apologetic. "I didn't have any reason to." He brightened. "But I must have seen it. Maybe you could get one of those police hypnotists?"

I thanked him and said we might get back to him later. In Las Vegas, there was not likely to be a police hypnotist. There might or might not be one in Santa Fe, and Salazar might or might not be interested in sending one up. Forensic hypnosis is not quite as widely regarded as it was a few years back, since it has developed that the subconscious mind is very, very cooperative and eager to please and will sometimes manufacture evidence that does not exist.

Which is to say, if we hypnotized Rex Lewis he might give us the licence plate number from the red Camaro, but on the other hand, if he genuinely hadn't noticed the red Camaro's license plate number and genuinely wanted to help—as he very clearly did—he might supply us the license plate number from his own car, or Salazar's car, or even my rented car, which was now sitting just where the red Camaro presumably had sat.

Somebody at the bank on the corner—a teller by the name of Becky Ortiz—claimed to recognize the composite.

Becky Ortiz was very nice and very young and very cooperative, and she might or might not have seen the man cashing a check last Friday at another teller's station. But whether she had or not she had absolutely no information that was of any use to us.

She didn't know his name or his account number or what kind of car he drove and she had never seen him with anybody, and the other teller didn't recognize the composite.

A jewelry store, also on the square. Two weeks ago the man in the composite had bought a ring for a girl—April, per photo lineup.

Depressingly, he hadn't written a check or used his MasterCard. The ring had to be sized for April; it was a size five and her ring finger was a size two. He'd paid a seventy-dollar deposit in cash and they'd left the ring to be picked up.

They'd left it in April's name.

The clerk showed me the ring. It was white gold with one diamond, which told me nothing of any current use.

As I exited the jewelry store, it did occur to me that he'd been doing quite a lot of hanging out on the square, which is more or less touristy rather than local, for somebody who was local, but then on the other hand he'd had April with him a lot of the time, and April wasn't local.

I went back to the police station and found Salazar eating a tuna fish sandwich at his desk. "You don't go out for lunch?" I commented.

He looked at me. "I've got six kids."

"Oh," I said. I have no idea how much small-town police chiefs get paid, and I wasn't about to ask, but it wasn't going to be enough to support a family of eight in any degree of comfort.

"Sometimes I go home for lunch," he added. "Right now I've got three kids with chicken pox."

I did not envy Maria Salazar. I also had once had three children with chicken pox at the same time. But in the first place I did not have three other children to cope with at the same time, and in the second place I did very little of the coping. I cravenly called my mother to babysit while I went and worked traffic, which happened to be my assignment at the time.

I *could* have taken leave and stayed with them myself. But I was needed at the police department.

Besides, my mother had already nursed four children through chicken pox. She was undoubtedly better at it than I was.

So I reasoned at the time. In retrospect I was a little bit ashamed of myself. When Little Whosit gets chicken pox I will stay home with him or her myself.

Maybe.

Or maybe not. I could decide that later; right now I had to worry about the present situation.

Between bites of sandwich—Salazar (or Maria, whom I was definitely going to have to meet) had thoughtfully provided tuna fish for me also—I explained what I had come across thus far.

Salazar nodded. "I think he's local," he said, "or at least he's lived here some. He damn sure knows northeastern New Mexico. He's not from out of state, at least not unless he's lived here a lot. Anyway, how'd he meet April if he wasn't local?"

"How'd he meet April if he *is* local?" I demanded. From the little I'd seen of the World College kids, they seemed rather clannish, unlike the students of Highlands University, who seemed to be congregating on every street corner doing or saying many assorted and doubtless absorbing things.

But then Highlands University draws almost entirely students from northern New Mexico, predominantly though not exclusively Hispanic students because of its outstanding Hispanic studies program. To them, Las Vegas, New Mexico, would be a familiar sort of a place even if they were new to the town itself, unlike the World College students, for whom it would be a totally foreign environment.

I said that to Salazar, and he nodded again. "But it's crossed my mind to wonder if he couldn't have been a student at Highlands."

"How would we find that out? You don't mean a current student, do you?"

Salazar shook his head. "No, I mean a former student. And I don't think there is any way to check it out. Not without a name or something. I mean, we could go look at the yearbooks, but what the hell good would that do? None that I know of. Somebody who knows him now could spot his yearbook picture and the composite. But I don't figure the composite is good enough you or I could spot the yearbook picture from it."

My guess was that Salazar was right.

"I guess we could call and see if they show him as a former student," he added. "But then if they do, with all this right to privacy stuff, we'd have to get a court order to get at the records, and then when we did get them it would probably be an out-of-date address."

"So what are you going to do?"

"Call Highlands, of course. But keep on with everything else at the same time."

He gulped coffee—from a Thermos cup—and answered the phone before it finished its first ring. "Salazar." He listened. "Yeah, put her through."

There's no need to recount what I heard. It's always confusing to hear only half a conversation. He wrote, asked a few questions, and said, "Thanks. There'll be somebody there to talk to you this afternoon."

He hung up and looked at me. "This is firm," he said. "A week ago April Greene of Las Vegas made an appointment with a women's clinic in Santa Fe for an abortion. The appointment was for this past Monday morning. She was there at seven o'clock; a man brought her in. They had a quarrel in the waiting room and the nurse thought she was going to have to call the police, but April managed to convince him she wasn't getting an abortion, she was just there for a checkup and a series of X-rays—the clinic does a lot of stuff besides abortions—and he quieted down. He said he was going across the street to get something to eat and he'd come back and pick her up. The nurse told April it wasn't a good idea to lie about it, and April shrugged and said he'd get over it. Apparently he did, because he picked her up around noon and they left together. She—the nurse that called me—says there should be more information in the records but she's got to get permission to give it to us. She says there shouldn't be a problem, with a murder investigation in progress."

"So I guess I get a trip to Santa Fe."

He looked at me. "You sure you feel like it? I mean, I don't want you to go into labor halfway between—"

"I'm two weeks off from my due date," I assured him.

"That doesn't always mean a hell of a lot."

Salazar was interesting me. Unlike most Hispanic men I knew—who at best tend to be considerably if unconsciously male supremacist—he clearly hadn't the slightest objection to my doing anything anybody else could do. His only worry was for my immediate safety in view of my advanced pregnancy.

But I didn't comment; I just watched as he went on through the note cards on his desk—apparently he took all his notes on index cards—and came up with one more. "You might as well check this out while you're there. There's probably nothing to it. It's an Emily Montrose—sounds from her voice like she's about sixty or so—who insists she knows the man in the composite. Before you take off let me make one quick phone call."

He dialed, while I brooded.

No, I don't very much like abortions; in fact, I don't like them at all, except in cases of rape, incest, and serious illness. But right now I was very, very sorry for April Greene. After that kind of experience she should have gone home and gone right to bed; apparently she had been dead set on convincing her boyfriend—whoever he was—that nothing was wrong, and they'd apparently gone up and had intercourse in the kiva before Hal and Lorie got to the park. I wondered how she'd talked him into the condom; I wondered how she'd explained the blood. But she had to have been hurting.

No wonder she had pain killers with her to give to Lorie. No wonder she'd been sympathetic with Lorie's cramps.

Was that why he had killed her, because she'd had the abortion?

If it was, why had he waited until the middle of the night, why hadn't he done it right then in the kiva?

Why—if that was his reason—had he taken Lorie with him? Lorie wasn't pregnant; Lorie hadn't had an abortion.

Had he taken Lorie with him at all? Or were we wrong about that?

I suddenly needed to make a couple of telephone calls too. "Be right back," I said, and Salazar, who was on hold, nodded.

There was a pay phone at a building across the street, and by now I had my telephone charge card number memorized, as well as a few other numbers.

No, Lorie was not at home.

No, Donna—who now was at home—had not heard from Lorie. She wanted, not unnaturally, to know what was going on. I told her we were working on it and I didn't have any real news yet and I'd call back when I did.

I could get away with that for now because the murder of a girl on the square in a small town in New Mexico—no matter how big the news is in New Mexico—is not going to turn up on television or in the papers in Texas.

How long I could continue to get away with it depended on how long Lorie stayed missing.

So if Lorie had started for home she hadn't gotten there yet, which was possible, and she hadn't called her mother, which was a lot less possible.

I needed to make one more telephone call. This one was to Julia Gonzales at the Wardance Motel.

And I was annoyed when I hung up. Why—when she knew we were investigating a murder—hadn't she thought it was important enough to tell me there was a lot of blood in the bed and a lot of blood in the bathroom?

She just thought the girl's period must have started without warning and she wasn't prepared with anything to use. "Some people are like that," Julia Gonzales told me. "Messy. Filthy. You wouldn't believe the way some of them leave motel rooms."

That was probably true.

I went back to the police station to find Salazar off the phone. "Autopsy report," he told me. "I hadn't called about it any sooner because it was pretty obvious how she died. We thought."

"We thought?"

"There are three possible causes of death," Salazar said. "For the proximate cause, I mean. The immediate cause is extravasation and hemorrhage. In English, she bled to death. The question is what from—she had a severed jugular vein, which definitely would have done it if nothing else did, she had a stab wound in her spleen, which certainly would have done it if nothing else did, but she was already in the process of bleeding to death from—there were a lot of long words, but it boils down to rough intercourse, possibly rape, real soon after an abortion. The son-of-a-bitch didn't care. He wasn't wearing anything that time. There was semen in her vagina and uterus."

"Her uterus?" I repeated.

Salazar nodded. "Ruptured uterus, of course," he added. I didn't say anything. I couldn't think of anything to say. Salazar was looking just about as horrified and disgusted as I felt.

"The time fits," he added. "Into the rest of it, I mean. The doctor figures she was killed maybe about two A.M. Raped maybe an hour before that. If she was raped in that motel room and then killed in the park—Damn it, somebody had to have doped that boy of yours, that's the only way he wouldn't wake up for a murder and then would wake up two hours later needing to pee—it must have been just wearing off then. Damn it, damn it, damn it, my patrol must have just missed the son of a bitch."

"That happens," I said.

"It happens," Salazar agreed. "It shouldn't but it does." After a couple of minutes he said, "Oh, hell," and handed me the cards with the names and addresses of the people I needed to talk with.

I went out to the car, feeling sick. From all we had been able to determine, April Greene was a shallow, silly, vain, manipulative girl.

But she hadn't deserved this.

It's about an hour drive down the interstate from Las Vegas to Santa Fe, through pretty country. Though I'm no geologist, I'd guess the Sangre de Cristos are a lot older mountains than the Rockies, which are what I generally think of as mountains. There was a lot of vegetation, a lot of weathered bluffs overgrown with trees and brush or sitting naked and exposed, depending on the amount of water available—this climate wasn't as dry as the southern New Mexico desert, but it was a long way from being as well-watered as the area near Los Alamos, where the mountains were virtually invisible in the overcoat of trees and vegetation. Here I could see why the Spaniards had named the mountain range as they did—Sangre de Cristo, Blood of Christ.

Water runoff from these hills would be a bright orange-red, really more orange than blood, but given the propensity of the Spaniards to give scriptural names to everything...

All right, I was maundering, mentally wandering. Of course I was. I didn't want to think about what had happened to April, and I didn't want to think about what might be happening to Lorie. I wanted to think about anything else I could come up with to think about.

The women's clinic was easy to find; it was just two blocks off the freeway exit my map told me to take, and the head nurse, Natalie Summers, was ready for me.

"You understand about confidentiality, I'm sure," she told me. When I nodded, she added, glancing at my nonexistent waistline. "Of course it's even more important for us." She didn't explain why, and I didn't ask. I was pretty sure I knew.

"But," she went on, "in this situation—when we know the patient has been murdered—well, we want to help the police all we can." She looked at my midsection again.

"I appreciate that," I said, trying to ignore her evident curiosity. In a minute she would ask me if I was sure I ought to be doing this kind of work in my present condition, and then I could reply. But I didn't want to try to answer a look.

"Well, here's the file," she said. "You want to just look through it, and then I can answer any questions?"

I am not an absolute world's champion at translating medicalese into English, but I have had some experience at it over the years, especially since getting into the Major Case Squad. The best that I could determine, April had been only about four weeks pregnant and a D and C had been performed. A D and C is used not only for early abortion, but also for assorted diagnostic and therapeutic purposes; in fact, I'd once had one myself in hopes that it would help the doctors to determine why I couldn't—at least then—become pregnant. (It had done no good whatever, any more than anything else had, and nobody had the slightest idea about why it was that I was having my first pregnancy in my early forties.)

The surgery, done under local anesthesia, had been uneventful, and April had been allowed to leave after an hour of rest. She'd been cautioned not to use tampons, not to have intercourse until at least a week after the bleeding stopped, to get plenty of rest, and to contact a doctor at once if she began to have fever. She'd been provided a prescription for pain medication, because she could be expected to have severe cramping for several days. She'd gone next door to the connected pharmacy to fill the prescription, and then she'd come back and sat on a chair in the waiting room with her feet up on another chair to read and wait for her boyfriend to come back and get her. While she was waiting, she put on a lot of makeup to mask her paleness, and when he arrived she strode out swinging her purse and smiling brightly.

That didn't all come from the report; some of it came from the memory of Natalie Summers and the memory of the receptionist, invited in to provide further information.

Both the receptionist and Natalie Summers easily picked the composite of the man in the red Camaro from a handful of composites of male Caucasians in their midtwenties. Both the receptionist and Natalie Summers easily picked April from a handful of photographs of thin young female Caucasians in their late teens. Not that there was any surprise to that; in view of the autopsy report, I would have been very surprised if they hadn't picked her.

Neither the receptionist nor Natalie Summers had seen the man's car or gotten the man's name. "We didn't have any reason to," the receptionist pointed out to me. "She put the bill on MasterCard."

I will try anything, if I think it might provide information.

So I went outside and asked questions of the picketers standing outside.

Of course there were picketers standing outside. How many places specializing in abortion in this country don't have picketers at least part of the time?

There was one picketer—one only—who had also been there on Monday. After much cajoling—my obvious pregnancy probably helped here—she did agree to look at pictures. She picked out April and said April had made a birdie—an obscene finger gesture—when she had tried to talk to April.

She picked out the composite of April's boyfriend and said he had stood out front and talked with the picketers for a few minutes, assuring them he was on their side, though he didn't, she added, say anything that made much sense. "Nuts on our side hinder our cause," she told me.

She had not seen his car.

She had not, of course, seen his license plate.

We were no better off than we had been when we started.

I got in the car and looked for the other address card.

EIGHT

EMILY MONTROSE lived toward the middle of Santa Fe. Of course I got lost. I always get lost in places I don't know, and I certainly didn't know these European-style streets, with no two streets quite parallel and no corners quite square. I could understand how tourists with time on their hands might enjoy meandering around, making new discoveries with nearly every step, but dammit, I was in a hurry. This downtown area didn't have much about it of either the United States—except glossy store windows and high prices—or Mexico—except the unlisped American Spanish. It had been designed, if not built, by Spaniards, and the narrow winding streets were pure Spanish.

I found the palace of the colonial governors, where the Indians selling jewelry were neatly arrayed on the porch precisely as Hal had told me, and I found the church with the miraculous staircase supposedly built by Saint Joseph, which Hal hadn't told me about, and I found a building that insisted it was the oldest house in New Mexico (but which now housed a pizza parlor), and I found a whole lot of people selling a whole lot of things, from magnificent hand-woven blankets to strings and wreaths of red chili peppers, almost all interesting and almost all expensive, but I did not find Emily Montrose's house. Or apartment. Or the street it was on. And my map confused me.

I found the present governmental buildings. I found some libraries and museums. I found some parks, and wondered which one Hal and Lorie had camped in. Some things I found two or three or four times, until finally I found the right street and found the apartment number that matched the one written on the card lying on the seat beside me.

As Salazar had guessed from her voice, she appeared to be in her midsixties. She was a totally conventional-looking woman, with totally conventional gray hair she probably got done once a week at the beauty school—the way it was set told me that—and slightly narrow blue eyes with brown-rimmed bifocals. Not that there is anything wrong with bifocals; at my age I expect to be in them soon myself. No, my objection was to her expression.

She was wearing a dress of some kind of synthetic, a string of imitation pearls, stockings, and closed-toe dress shoes. Apparently meeting a police officer was an occasion in her life.

Maybe she expected a male police officer.

She led me into a room that had taken no note whatever of the Spanish/Southwestern ambience all around her; her maple and chintz and the uninspired seascape over the couch would have been more at home in New England. She offered me an upholstered chair that was in fact somewhat too deep and somewhat too low for comfort, especially now, but she was trying to be nice and I gritted my mental teeth and sat in it.

"And *you're a policeman*?" she said to me in a tone more hostile than admiring.

"Police officer," I corrected. A policeman I obviously am not, but policeperson is the most detestable neologism I have ever heard. I mean, why invent a grotesque nongendered word when a perfectly good nongendered word already exists?

"But isn't it *depressing*? All that blood?"

"I'm quite sure nurses see far more blood than I do."

"But it just seems so unladylike. And it can't be good for your baby. Why, when I was expecting Jillie, I had to rest four hours every afternoon."

"Then I must be very fortunate to be so healthy."

She chirped conventionally for a while longer, to make sure I knew how very much she disapproved of my profession. That duty done, she then offered me coffee, iced tea, pie, and cookies. I waved photographs at her and regretfully she abandoned her imitation of hospitality and got down to business.

"Yes, this one," she told me, perched gingerly on the edge of the piano bench looking through the photographs of composites. "This is the one that was on the television."

"And you recognize him?"

"Oh yes. Just a minute." She got up and headed for another room again, and I hoped she wasn't going to come back with something else to offer me. About all she hadn't come up with yet was a blanket to cover my knees.

But she returned with a white-covered book; after a second I recognized it as that type of photograph album that is sold for wedding pictures. She opened it. "My daughter Jill and her ex-husband," she said, and handed it to me.

I couldn't say—not for sure—that the man in the photograph was the man in the composite. But he looked enough like the composite to be well worth checking out.

"What's his name?"

She looked a little surprised. "You don't know that?"

"No, ma'am, that's why we put the composite on television, in hopes of getting his name."

"Oh, well, it's Darren Fletcher, of course. But Jillie always called him Sugar, while—oh, you know, before they broke up."

That clinches it, I thought. If she thinks he's Darren Fletcher and the motel registration card says he's Darren Fletcher—but Sugar? "Why was that?" I asked.

"The breakup? It was because—"

"No, I mean why did she call him Sugar?"

"Oh, well, he used to box, you know."

"Oh?"

"Yes, sort of semipro. He never was very good at it, I don't think. But those boxers, you know, they have some sort of *thing* about that nickname Sugar. And he boxed as Sugar Fletcher."

"Okay, you said he's your daughter's ex-husband, that right?" Ione had said April's dreamboat was married.

"Well—you could say that."

"Yes, but I need to know exactly. Is he her husband or her former husband?"

"Well, they're separated, you know." Her expression was exactly as if she had bitten an extra-sour lemon. "When I was a girl people just didn't *do* that sort of thing. You got married and you *stayed* married."

I decided getting into a philosophic discussion of human nature probably wouldn't be the best idea. She went on talking.

"Jillie is having an awful time with him, he just pesters her and pesters her to come back to him."

"Do you know why she doesn't want to?"

"Oh, well, she says he used to hit her and that sort of thing. But you know men, they will be men."

"Yes indeed they will. So she left him because he was abusing her?"

"Well, that's what she *said*."

"But you're not sure you believe it."

"Oh, I didn't say *that*. But such a nice-looking young man—you could tell by looking he came from a nice family, and such fine *teeth*—"

Just what every woman needs, I thought. He can be as worthless and abusive as he wants to be, so long as he has a nice Anglo-Saxon name and Jimmy Carter teeth. "All right," I said, "I need to be making some notes. Let's see, you said his name is Darren Fletcher, that right? Is that Darren with an *e* or an *i*." I was purposely re-covering steps I'd already covered, to try to get her a little more at ease. I already knew it was *Darren*, not *Darrin*, because I'd seen the way he signed the motel registration card. And a man might change his name, but it was doubtful that he'd change the way he spelled his name.

"With an *e*," she assured me. "I'm sure of that."

"And he's your daughter's husband but he's separated from her?"

"That's right."

"Any children?" I was remembering what else Ione had told me.

"Yes, a little boy, Scotty. He's just six months old. A beautiful baby." She beamed at me, a conventionalized grandmotherly expression with a sort of coldness behind it that bothered me.

"What kind of work does he do?" I asked. "Darren, I mean?"

"He doesn't have a regular job. He makes handicrafts and that sort of thing and sells them at fairs and flea markets."

"What sort of handicrafts?"

"Just things," she said vaguely. "Handicrafts."

"Leather doodads, things like that?"

"Things like that. It seemed like an awfully peculiar job for a grown man. But Jillie said he started it when he was in the hospital for a long time after a boxing injury, and he was quite good at it. I suppose he'd have done something else later."

Most likely I had just found the explanation for April's anklet. One small problem cleared up. "Where does he live?" I asked.

"You know, I just don't know where he *does* live."

"Where did he live when he was married to your daughter?"

"Why, with her, of course."

"All right, where does *she* live?"

"In Las Vegas." She gave me the address.

"I see. And how long did they live there?"

"Oh, well, she still lives there, you see."

"Yes, you told me that," I said, striving for patience. "But how long did they both live there?"

"Oh, about six months. Well, let me think." She stopped to count on her fingers. "Yes, that would be about right. They got married early in January and then Darren moved out about the end of August."

"They got married early in January and Darren moved out in August and the baby is six months old—"

"You needn't think *that*," she said, looking more than ever as if she had bitten a sour lemon.

"I needn't think what?"

"There wasn't anything *wrong*. Little Scotty was just a month premature, that's all."

"Oh, dear! Mrs. Montrose, I'm dreadfully sorry, I wasn't implying a thing." I assured her. "I was just trying to get dates straight in my mind, that's all."

"Well, I wouldn't want you to think—"

"I wasn't. Truly I wasn't."

But of course I was. Because Darren Fletcher—and by now it seemed reasonably certain Darren Fletcher was Darren Fletcher—wanted to marry April because she was pregnant. Had he also wanted to marry "Jillie" because she was pregnant? It certainly wasn't impossible.

But why, if he lived in Las Vegas for six months, hadn't he been in the telephone book? "Mrs. Montrose," I asked, "was the telephone and so forth in his name?"

"What do you mean? I never saw their bills! Are you suggesting I would *pry*?"

"I mean—oh, let's try it this way. Did he and Jill get the house together, or had he or Jill either one already been living in it before they got married?"

"Oh, well, it's Jillie's house. Not that she *owns* it, I mean, I don't think women ought to own houses, do you? It needs a man, but she was renting it. She's going to school there, at that Highlands University. I'm sure I don't know why, all those Chicanos there, and I'm sure she could have gotten a much better education at..."

Never mind the rest of it. Nothing else was any use except that we did manage to establish his date of birth; the rest of the conversation served only to make it clearer and clearer to me that Emily Montrose's brain, such as it was, was afloat on a billowing sea of prejudice and stereotype, and any attempt to dissuade her from the stereotypes would have been totally futile, even though several of her ideas were mutually contradictory.

When I finally managed to escape, I went to a pay telephone and called Salazar. "Fletcher," he said thoughtfully, when I gave him the address. "Yeah, I ought to remember that one. We've gotten several disorderly calls to it, woman's ex out there raising sand, you know how that goes."

I certainly know how that goes, as does anybody who's been on any police department more than about two months. Most people think that the most dangerous call a police officer can get is to a robbery or a murder. It isn't. Almost every year more police officers across the United States are seriously injured or killed on calls to domestic quarrels than for any other single reason.

So an address that you get a lot of domestic calls to is flagged. That means that the dispatcher, when issuing the call, warns the officer that it is a repeat address and should be approached with extreme caution.

Not that I suppose you'd need a flagged address in a town this size; probably everybody on the department would remember the addresses you'd have to flag in a bigger place.

"I'll go on over there and check it out," Salazar said. "You feeling all right?"

"Of course I'm feeling all right. Why wouldn't I be?"

"Just thought I'd ask. Begay came in and got Hal and they're both back out prowling around with pictures of the composite."

"So you wanted to be sure I was feeling okay before you told me," I said.

"Well," Salazar said, and let it go at that.

"Whose idea was it? Hal's, I suppose?"

"Actually it was Begay's. He's decided he likes Hal."

"Anything else you want me to check on in Santa Fe?" I asked, deciding not to comment on the suggestion that Begay now liked Hal.

"Naah, come on in. I'll call NCIC and add what you got."

So I drove back up to Las Vegas, not taking as much note of the scenery as I had done on the way down, and found Salazar in his office waiting for me.

"She wasn't there," he told me.

"Who, Jill Fletcher? Well, she might be in class. Her mother said she's a student."

"She doesn't live there anymore," he corrected himself. "The neighbors told me she'd moved about two months ago."

"Without telling her mother?"

"From what you tell me about the mother—"

"Well, that's true," I admitted.

"But I checked at the university," he added, "and she's still enrolled there. He dropped out last fall. For what that's worth."

"Oh?"

"He was a PE major. Not on a sports scholarship. I did get that much."

"But they wouldn't give you either address?"

"Right. So I've got calls in to all the utilities. Even if she's in a 'utilities paid' apartment she ought to at least have a phone in her own name."

"If she's got a phone."

"Why wouldn't she have a phone?"

"If she's divorced or separated and supporting a child and going to school—"

"Oh. Yeah. I didn't think of that. You may be right."

"I am right."

"Okay, you are right." His telephone rang, and he grabbed it. After a moment of writing on an index card, he hung up. "Electric company. We've got an address. You want to go with me?"

"I guess. Is Hal still out with Begay?"

"Yep. Begay's not married, and when he gets his teeth into something..."

"I'm like that myself. My husband gets mad at me sometimes for it."

"As I said, he's not married. Anyhow, yeah, they're still out and I guess they'll be in when they get in. So. I say again. You want to go over there with me?"

"I said yes."

In a town the size of Las Vegas, no place is very far from any other place. It was less than ten minutes before Salazar parked his police car in front of a ramshackle adobe house. The lawn, such as it was, had not been mowed lately, and four newspapers lay on the front porch. The mailbox bristled with brochures, catalogs, and flyers, and as we walked up toward the front porch I could hear two things: flies buzzing and a baby crying.

Not a baby crying normally. The thin, hopeless wail of a neglected baby, a baby half-starved and forgotten. The sound I'd heard more than once when I was in uniform division. The mother wasn't there.

No woman could listen to that and not do something about it. The mother wasn't there or—

Or.

The mother—or somebody—was there. And would leave only in a body bag.

The smell, this close, was obvious. Why hadn't somebody called already? Why hadn't the mail carrier reported it? Why hadn't a neighbor called the police? How many days had the baby—Scotty—been crying?

Salazar hit the unscreened front door with his shoulder and went on going. He didn't stop to warn me not to come in; he had more respect for me than that, or, as the father of six children, he was going to get to that baby before he thought about anything else. I had no idea which; I just went with him.

The heat was turned up; it must have been eighty-five degrees in there, and Salazar left the front door open as he headed for the room from which the wailing was coming. He stopped, briefly, on the threshold of that room.

I had a strange feeling of déjà vu; several times before I have gone into a house where someone had been dead for a long time; several times before I have found a baby in the room with a corpse. But never before have I found a baby in a room with a corpse several days dead.

There were six bottles in the bed; at a guess, three or four of them had held milk, and two or three had held water. Somebody had expected the baby would be found within a day or two. But the bottles were all empty now, long empty, and why that baby was still alive was more than I could guess. He needed a diaper change, but he needed milk more than that. I grabbed one of the bottles, totally oblivious to any evidence I might be destroying—and right then I wouldn't have cared if I had thought of it—and headed for the kitchen.

When I got back with the formula—there was powdered Enfamil in the kitchen—Salazar had the baby out of the crib, into the bathroom, washed and rediapered. "You work fast," I told him.

"Yeah," he said, and handed the baby to me.

Juggling baby and bottle with less expertise than I would like to claim—my last baby is sixteen years old, and I don't spend as much time with my grandbaby as I would like to—I followed Salazar back into the bedroom.

I had to feed the baby holding him, because I wasn't going to go out into the living room and leave Salazar to study this scene by himself, and I certainly wasn't going to sit down on the floor, which was somewhat bloody, or on the bed. Which was occupied.

I had seen Jill Fletcher's wedding picture not four hours ago, and the wedding picture had been taken not much over a year before. But I couldn't, now, say from the pictures that this was Jill Fletcher. I doubted anybody could. She was, at a guess, five days dead. Four at least. Four or five days dead in a very hot room.

Once smelled, that odor is never forgotten. Here it was horribly strong; when I got back to the motel room I'd have to shampoo with lemon shampoo, and brush my teeth, gargle, and wash my clothes in the wash basin before I even picked them up to take them out to a Laundromat. And even then I'd be tasting it in the back of my mouth for days and days and days.

At least Salazar wasn't trying to find any air freshener spray. No spray can mask it, and all that happens is you get to hate whatever spray somebody tried to use because its smell becomes associated in your mind with that smell.

Predictably, he said, "Hell."

Then he varied it. "Hell and damnation."

In Fort Worth, it would now be time to call for the lab crew to photograph and collect evidence. It was reasonable to assume that there was no lab crew here.

Salazar opened the window, then, rethinking, he closed it again. He headed out the front door, returning with the same small camera and the brief-case-sized evidence collection kit he'd used at Bandelier. He took ten pictures, fast. Then he got a packet of index cards out of the briefcase and began, quite methodically, to take notes.

The baby stopped sucking on the bottle and I held him up to burp him. He vomited down my back.

"That's just what we needed," Salazar muttered.

"So? What do you expect me to do about it?" I demanded.

"There ain't much you can do, now is there? I don't know. Get a towel or something."

"Talk about locking the barn door..." I growled, and got a towel.

Salazar had to put down his note cards and pen and accompany me into the bathroom to mop my shoulder, not that that did much good in terms of getting rid of odor. The baby commenced howling again.

Maybe I should not try to give him milk right now. Maybe he couldn't handle milk until he was a little rehydrated. Maybe I should give him water. Sugar water?

Taking the baby with me, leaving Salazar taking notes, I went to look in the refrigerator.

There was a Seven-Up in there. That would be too fizzy, too much sugar, but if I shook it up and let the bubbles subside a few times and then diluted it half and half with water...

I went back into the bedroom, with the baby drinking diluted Seven-Up, and said, "Salazar?"

"Yeah?"

"Don't you think we ought to call an ambulance for this baby?"

He stopped and looked at me. "No," he said.

"Why?"

"Because I don't want an ambulance here yet. They'll want to come tramping through getting into things."

"Not if you don't let them in until—"

He looked at me again. "Deb," he said.

"Yeah?"

"How many cars you think I got on the road?"

"I don't know. How many?"

"Two. And I want them *on* the road, not over here gawking. Get it on the radio and I'll have—"

"But the baby—"

"Is not going anywhere. Kids are durable."

I've said that myself enough times, and I knew he was right. Newborn babies were dug out of the wreckage of hospitals after the Mexico City earthquake as late as seven and eight days after the quake, still alive and howling. In some of those cases the baby had been buried by the quake only moments after birth, and had never had any milk or water. He was right. This baby wasn't going anywhere. Already his howl, when he temporarily lost the nipple, was perceptibly louder and his little body was cooler. The Seven-Up had been the right idea. The liquid was going practically right into his bloodstream.

I supposed that grandmother in Santa Fe would wind up raising him, poor kid. Darren Fletcher, however much he might claim to love kids, was certainly never going to get this one back, and it was doubtful that a court would award the baby to Fletcher's parents, whoever they might happen to be. Which left Emily Montrose. Unless the baby was real lucky and she decided she didn't want him and let him be adopted.

"Salazar?" I said.

"Yeah?"

"You know what's funny about this?"

He sat back on his heels and stared at me. "If anything is I'd sure as hell like to know what."

"I know a Darren Fletcher."

"Not this one?"

"No. The Darren Fletcher I know is an FBI agent."

Involuntarily Salazar chuckled. "That'd be the shits, wouldn't it? Any kin, you think?"

"I certainly hope not. I mean, really. I'm not any crazier about the FBI than the next cop, but really—"

"Okay. You're right. They're on our side. I hope not too."

He continued writing, and I looked around. I had my hands full; I couldn't stop and take notes, but if this ever came to trial I too was going to have to testify. Not about what I had smelled, which was utterly indescribable, but about what I had seen and what I had done.

Jill lay on her back on the bed, in a blue chiffon nightgown and a quilted blue bedjacket. That said she was not the one who had turned up the heat so high; women wear bedjackets because the manufacturers of nightclothes, who provide sleeves for men, think women should be perfectly comfortable all night with nothing but a pair of thin lace straps between their shoulders and the universe. In the summer, if the air-conditioning is not turned too cold, those straps are enough. But in the winter, for anybody with any regard at all for her heating bill, something else is definitely required.

Besides, a woman who couldn't afford a telephone wouldn't be able to afford to turn the heat up to ninety.

Judging from the books on her bedside table, she was a sociology major, and at least a junior. Judging from the grade I could see on an essay that had fallen or been thrown to the floor, she was a good student. Judging from the general condition of the house and the clothes (both hers and the baby's), she'd been doing the best she could with what she had. She hadn't deserved to die like this. For a moment I felt an immense sorrow for the waste of her potential.

But cops can't afford emotion. Look for facts.

She was lying on the bed on her back in a blue chiffon nighty with white lace straps and bare feet. Her throat had been cut almost to her spine. There were several more stab wounds in her abdomen, and there were numerous defense wounds on the backs of her hands, those wounds I had looked for and found on April's hands.

Like April, Jill had been awake. She had tried to fight. But like April, she had been a small woman. She hadn't stood any chance at all against an ex-boxer armed with...

What was he armed with?

He didn't have Harry's knife, not then.

"Salazar," I said, "where's the knife?"

He looked up at me. "What did you say?"

"The knife. Where's the knife? He didn't have my husband's knife, not when he was here; Hal hadn't even gotten here yet. So where's the knife he used?"

Salazar stood up, looked around.

There was no knife on the floor, on the bed, on any visible surface. Salazar yanked the cover up and looked under the bed. "Check the kitchen," he told me.

Unless he'd washed it and put it back in the knife drawer while he was making the baby formula, which didn't seem very likely, the knife wasn't in the kitchen. It also was not in the living room. It also was not, Salazar told me, in the bathroom.

"He's got it with him, then," I said. "He's got Lorie and he's got the knife."

"What the hell difference you think that makes?" Salazar said. "If he didn't have that knife he'd just get another. Oh, shit. Deb, that baby's asleep. Put him down and go start looking for address books."

"No search warrant—"

"Go start looking for address books."

I didn't want to put the baby back down in that filthy crib. But I picked the cleanest corner of it and put him down anyway, to start looking for address books.

NINE

THE MOST LIKELY PLACE to look for an address book seemed to be in a large pile of magazines and assorted papers on the right-hand side of the threadbare beigeish couch in the claustrophobically small living room. Turning on what light there was and mentally cursing the darkness, I set to work.

Ten minutes later—after one pause for going to the bathroom, which required both me and Salazar to stop what we were doing to check the bathroom for usable evidence—I knew that Jill Fletcher subscribed to *Newsweek*, occasionally bought *McCalls*, and had made A on her last three papers for Sociology 368. I knew that she was a confirmed reader of grocery store tabloids (what my husband Harry calls "the untruth sheets") and that she had started, but never finished, a furious letter to President Reagan on the occasion of his having met, in Moscow, with Native American tribal leaders who had been unable to arrange to meet him at home. Reagan had later expressed himself as being puzzled by what their complaint was, with the nice reservations to live on and the nice Bureau of Indian Affairs to take care of them, and Jill had expressed her opinion.

I turned over a *National Enquirer* and found tucked beneath it an imitation leather daybook, the kind that starts in September and ends in August so as to get the entire academic year in one book. It had room for notes, assignments, and telephone numbers and addresses. Unfortunately, the address section, to which I of course turned first, was blank. Well, it wasn't completely blank; she had used it not to write down names and addresses but to draw up an elaborate chart of how much weight she would lose if she stuck to whatever diet she was on for X number of weeks. I recognized the chart at once, having drawn up similar schedules myself (though not in the address book section of my daybook).

Well, some people keep track of addresses on the day page, as soon as they get the address, until they have time to transfer them to their regular address book. Hopefully I began leafing through the daily pages.

I learned what her assignments had been, how she had gone about figuring the due date for her baby. (He arrived two weeks early, which made me a little nervous. On my own account, that is, not on her account; I had long since decided that Emily Montrose's rather hysterical insistence that Jill's baby had

been a month premature was no more than a case of
the lady doth protest too much.)

I did not, however, find out anything at all that
might help to locate her husband or ex-husband, as
the case may be, and besides that I was getting an
awful backache from crouching over this stuff with
my head too close to it, a proximity dictated by the
incurable darkness in the room. Abandoning the
daybook at the first week in February, I returned to
the pile of papers—and heard a screech of brakes
outside.

There was no front window in this adobe house. I
ran for the front door, and as I saw a red car complete a U-turn (running over a curb and an adjoining yard—I cannot say lawn—in the process) Salazar
charged past me. Jumping rather than stepping off
the front threshold, he hit the ground running and
unsnapping the strap to his pistol at the same time.
Seconds later the black-and-white Ford peeled out
and took off after the red car.

As I had expected to spend the rest of the afternoon with Salazar, I had not brought the walkie-
talkie I had been using earlier. There was no telephone in the house, and I did not think that I wanted
to visit with or try to borrow a telephone from
neighbors who could listen to a baby cry for four or

five days without ever going to find out what was going on.

The upshot of it was that I not only had no way to call and ask somebody to come and get the baby and me, I did not even have any way to keep track of what was going on.

What did I do?

I did the logical thing. I went to the bathroom, checked the baby, and then returned to the stack of papers and resumed looking for address books, letters, or anything else that might help us to locate the permanent or even any good temporary address for Darren Fletcher. Of course the situation was not as critical as it would have been if we had had to locate the address book before we knew the victim's next-of-kin, but still . . .

There were two possibilities, I decided a moment later. Either Jill was normally tidy and this corner was where she stuck everything she had no other place for, or else she was chronically *un*tidy and she had bundled all the clutter into this one spot in a great hurry because she was expecting guests.

I was not expecting guests. Not while I was alone in a house with a dead woman and no telephone. But somebody was fumbling at the front door. I do not mind telling you that I was backed against the wall with my hand on my pistol butt when Salazar came back in, looking extremely disgusted. "I lost him," he reported.

"Oh?"

"Well, I didn't really lose him. I never did have him to start with. He had too much of a lead and my car hasn't exactly got the greatest engine in the state of New Mexico. Anyway I have city, county, and state people looking for him. And a hell of a lot of chance they have of finding him," he added bitterly.

"What makes you say that?"

"You think about it. How many red Camaros with young white male drivers do you think there are on the road? And we don't even know the fu— we don't even know the damned license tag number or what state... How are they going to find him? How are *we* going to find him? Oh, hell." He turned his back on me and strode back into the bedroom, where I followed just in time to see him crawling under the bed.

A chief of police who is in the process of crawling under a bed is best left alone, I decided, and went quietly to the bathroom before returning to my own task of trying to find an address book and trying to think—to work out discrepancies.

If she weren't normally tidy except for this one spot—and she'd certainly have every reason not to be; the combination of earning a living, caring for a newborn baby still small enough to demand a lot of care in the middle of the night, and maintaining good grades in school must have been exhausting—then what guest had she been expecting the day she was killed? Because if it was a girlfriend she could expect the girlfriend to understand; you just say "Pardon the wreckage, I was up all night with the baby," and the girlfriend most likely will not only sympathize, she'll even offer to help clean it up. So it wasn't a girlfriend. And it certainly couldn't be her mother because her mother hadn't even given us a good address and therefore almost certainly did not know where Jill was living now. So if it wasn't a girlfriend and it wasn't her mother...

I got up and went back to the bedroom again. "Salazar?"

"Yeah?" His voice sounded somewhat muffled. I wondered what he thought he was going to find under the bed.

"Suppose Montrose was lying?"

Salazar backed out from under the bed, his appearance not at all improved by a collection of animal hair and dust bunnies and a number of shiny black flakes of dried blood. "Suppose Montrose was lying about what?" He sounded tired.

"Think about it," I said. "We have two different stories."

"We have two different stories about *what*?" he yelled.

Honestly, he is as bad as Harry. Men accuse me of not making sense because they won't listen to me explain how I figured out whatever it is I figured out. "Ione told us," I said, with as much dignity as I could muster, "that Fletcher 'didn't like' his wife. Now, admittedly that was not what you'd call first-hand testimony; it was what April told Ione that Fletcher had told her, but all the same, it clashes thoroughly with Montrose insisting that Jill threw Fletcher out and he wanted to come back."

"Let me get this straight," he said, absentmindedly dusting his uniform. "We have two conflicting stories. Ione told us that Fletcher left Jill and Montrose told us that Jill threw Fletcher out. They can't both be right. Well, if I had to pick one I'd say I'd buy Montrose's story. I mean, look, if the guy was beating her—"

"But that's Montrose's story too," I argued.

Salazar looked pointedly at the body on the bed.

"Oh, I know, if he killed her it stands to reason he'd beat her too, but that's not really certain. Anyway, even if he was, some women—"

"Are masochists," Salazar said drily. "Are you saying Jill was?"

"I didn't say anybody was. Most women who stay with wife beaters do it because they honestly don't have any way to fend for themselves and their children, or at least they think they don't, and—"

"She doesn't fall into that category," Salazar interrupted. "She's obviously perfectly self-supporting."

"Or, I was going to say, their self-esteem is so low they're convinced nobody else could ever love them."

"I'd say she had every reason to have high self-esteem," Salazar argued. "Have you seen the *grades* that girl was making?"

"You didn't meet her mother. I did. That woman could make Arnold Schwarzenegger feel helpless."

"Okay," Salazar said, "suppose you're right. Suppose he did leave her instead of the other way around. Just exactly how much difference does that make to this investigation?"

"Come in the kitchen and I'll show you," I said. I checked the baby, who had been quiet a good long time, but he was definitely only asleep; his little chest was rising and falling steadily, and I headed for the tiny, cluttered kitchen with Salazar right behind me.

He regarded the stove, the counter. "So?" he said. "So she didn't wash the dishes. So what?"

"Salazar, she had a dinner guest, can't you tell?"

"No, and I don't know how you can tell, either."

"Look at the *pan*! Look at what-all she's got out on the counter. She made chicken-fried steak. Now, do you really think she would be buying steak for herself, with what her finances appear to have been? And even if she did, would she have used two plates? Look, she had chicken-fried steak, French fries, green salad, apple pie—that's homemade apple pie. She had a guest, and it was a guest that mattered a lot to her."

"That's a moldy mess, how in the hell do you think you can tell—"

"Just take my word for it, okay?"

He regarded the counter glumly. "All right, I will concede that in culinary matters you are far more likely to be an expert than I am. I will take your word for it that she had chicken-fried steak, French fries, salad, and apple pie, and that she had a guest. Are you assuming that the guest was Fletcher?"

"You have a counter-assumption? Look, she had to wash dishes after this meal before she could make another meal, because she had used up practically every pan and dish she owned. But the dishes never got washed and there is no indication that any meal after that ever got prepared. So what do you want to bet—"

"That was the last meal she ate? You're probably right. All right, so she had a male dinner guest and—"

"She had a male dinner guest and she never washed the dishes after it. Why? Because she didn't feel like it, or because she was lying on the bed dead? Because her dinner guest was the one who killed her?"

"I gather that you are suggesting that I should dust the silverware and glasses and so forth for fingerprints?"

"I would," I said rather spitefully. "If it were my—"

"It is *not* your case. But you're probably right. Let me finish up in the other room. You keep up with what you were doing."

I went to the bathroom; when I came out Salazar was back under the bed. I don't know what he thought he was doing there. I returned to the pile of papers. "Salazar," I called five minutes later.

"I'm *busy*. If you want me you'll have to come here."

"I can't. I'm buried under a pile of newspapers."

"Oh, hell." The banging that he was doing eloquently telling me that it was very inconvenient, he disengaged himself from the bedsprings and came into the living room. "What is it? Look, I'm busy.

There's a stash on the underside of the bed. I'm trying to figure out what—"

I handed him a newspaper that had an advertisement circled in green ink. "A motive."

Want the best for your baby and can't provide it? Help us complete our family. Professional couple desire to adopt healthy white infant, male preferred. Your baby will have all the advantages two loving parents in good financial shape can provide. Strictly legal.

There was a telephone number, a 415 area code. "That's San Francisco," I told him.

"What the hell?" Salazar said. "Look, this is stupid. She couldn't give that baby up for adoption without his consent, not if he's on the birth certificate as father."

"You know that and I know that," I agreed. "And with her a sociology major, chances are she knew it. But what's to say she meant to do it to start with? Maybe she was just threatening—you come back to me or else . . ."

"Has anybody ever told you you have a vivid imagination?"

"Frequently." In fact that is my besetting sin as a police officer; I tend to jump to conclusions. But I don't try to make a case on my assumptions; I use my assumptions to guide my investigation, and well over half the time those conclusions I had jumped to without evidence turn out, when the evidence turns up, to be absolutely correct.

"Shit," Salazar said. That, together with *hell*, seemed to be his favorite word. "Okay, he's got a wife he's separated from—who left who doesn't really matter at this point—and she's threatening to let their baby be adopted out. And he's got a girlfriend who's just told him she's pregnant. If that's what happened then he'd have reason enough to believe he had problems. He *did* have problems. Now our only problem besides finding him and rescuing Lorie is, we don't have any evidence that that's what happened. Or, for that matter, that it didn't. Or if it didn't what did."

"We've got plenty of evidence that he knew April was pregnant."

"Okay, but that's all we've got evidence for."

"We can prove that he was her—Jill's—dinner guest."

"By fingerprints on the dinner knife, right. Look, Deb, go hunt an address book and leave me to my work, okay?"

So he didn't like my theory. Well, I couldn't help that. It was the best theory I could come up with right now and I thought it was a pretty good one myself.

I went back to looking for an address book and, surprise, surprise, I found one.

Darren Fletcher's most recent addresses—there were four others crossed out—was in Flagstaff. Address and telephone number both. So Darren, who sold leather doodads at flea markets, could afford a telephone as well as a lot of travel between Arizona and New Mexico? That was interesting. What else did Darren sell besides leather doodads at flea markets?

Maybe I was being cynical. Maybe Darren Fletcher had a rich daddy who supported him, although not very many scions of rich daddies wind up going to college at Highlands University in Las Vegas, New Mexico. It is decidedly a school for hard-working idealistic working-class students.

Maybe I think too much.

I took the address book to Salazar, who by now was out from under the bed. "The stash was where he stored the scrap leather left from leatherwork," he reported disgustedly. "I turned it over piece by piece. Not a trace of contraband. He probably forgot about it when he moved out." To cheer him up I thrust the address book at him; he accepted it with a rather pleased expression and at once reached for his walkie-talkie, which he had previously removed from his belt and set on the dresser. "Car one to headquarters," he told it.

"Headquarters, go ahead."

I checked the baby again while they talked. He was still asleep, and he didn't feel feverish anymore. Of course we had long since turned the heat down to something approaching normal, and I thought maybe I had better find a blanket and cover him. We were wearing street clothes and working, so we were warm enough, but asleep in nothing but a diaper...

"Call the Arizona Department of Motor Vehicles and get automobile registration for Darren Fletcher, address"—he read the address from the book and, for good measure, added the previous Arizona addresses—"Also have Flagstaff PD ride over and just check to be sure he's not at home."

"Ten-four."

Salazar put the radio down and Scotty Fletcher woke up and began to howl. I picked him up and he hushed.

"Oh, shit," Salazar said. He picked up the radio again. "Headquarters."

"Go ahead."

"Call this telephone number and find out if a Jill Fletcher had called them about maybe adopting her baby. Be real tactful; be sure they don't think you think they're doing anything wrong. But I need the information fast."

While he was talking I changed the baby and put him back down. Of course he instantly resumed howling.

"What are you doing?" Salazar asked.

"I'm going to the bathroom again," I told him, "and then I'm going to make a bottle."

He eyed me. "You're going to the bathroom *again*?" He glanced at his watch.

"Yes," I said, deliberately adopting a tone that practically dared him to say anything else about it.

By the time I got out of the bathroom and then back from the kitchen, Salazar was on the radio with the dispatcher, who was telling him that she'd just talked with a Joy Cook in San Francisco, who confirmed that she and her husband had been discussing adopting Jill Fletcher's six-month-old baby, but only, she'd assured the dispatcher, if they could do it legally. She said Jill had told her she was afraid of the baby's father and didn't think the baby was safe. Was the baby safe, Mrs. Cook had asked the dispatcher, who had promised to call back and let her know.

"Thanks," Salazar said. "You can tell her the baby's safe." He turned to look at the baby, who was in the process of putting away the contents of the new

bottle as rapidly as possible. "This is stupid," he told
me. "It doesn't make sense to try to work like this."

I didn't tell him I agreed with him. But maybe it
was pretty obvious, because he called headquarters
again. "Have North Car meet me at this address.
Call welfare and have them locate an emergency fos-
ter parent to meet me at headquarters to take charge
of a six-month-old baby. And have the next shift
come in early," he added. "We're short-handed today."

"Ten-four."

North Car turned out to be an Anglo in his midtwenties whose name tag said PHILLIPS. Salazar
started telling him what he needed to be extra careful about while guarding the crime scene, because we
were getting ready to leave.

As far as I was concerned, it was high time and
then some. Thing is, if you stay in a very bad smell
long enough your olfactory nerves go numb, or
something like that; at any rate, you eventually quit
smelling it until after you've been out in the fresh air
and then you can smell it on yourself, in your hair
(hair shafts are hollow, and smells get in there and
stay), and in the back of your throat and so forth.
Salazar, for the most part, was staying in there in the
bedroom, right by the smell, so he had long since quit
smelling it. But I was going in and out, in and out,

because unfortunately the bathroom was off the bedroom, and every time I went in there the smell hit me again. Let's face it, I was not in optimum physical condition to cope with any kind of stress, let alone the smell of a five-day corpse.

Or four-day. Or whatever it was.

While Salazar was waiting for, and then instructing, North Car, I looked through the daybook again. I had given up on it at some point in February; now I was looking for—and through—March.

And there it was. On Friday, the day before, Hal and Lorie had taken off on this excursion of theirs. *Darren dinner 5:30.* And if she was having some other Darren over for dinner, and it was some other Darren that murdered her, well, I just didn't believe it, that's all.

Triumphantly I put the daybook into Salazar's hands; he stopped talking with Phillips long enough to glance down at the entry and nod, and then he told Phillips to be on close guard because the killer might try to come back for the baby.

And we left with the baby. After I went to the bathroom one more time.

A block from the house, Salazar slowed up beside a Seven-11. "What's that?" he muttered.

"What's what?" And then I saw what he was looking at. A red Camaro was backed in at the side of the store, its license plate artfully smeared with mud. Nobody was visible in the car. Salazar parked at the next closest available parking spot—which was about four cars away toward the front of the store—and notified the dispatcher where we were before he got out of the car. He didn't ask for backups. Probably he didn't have any to send for.

I had not even seen the driver, much less any possible passenger, when the red car took off from the front of the house. So I still didn't know whether Lorie was with him or not. I was reasonably sure that if he didn't have her he knew where she was, but getting him to tell might not be easy.

I wished I did not have to worry about Lorie. I couldn't help wondering what I was going to tell her mother if I could not bring her home.

Meanwhile I was watching Salazar head cautiously for the front door of the Seven-11, leaving the red Camaro behind and only semiguarded by me. I mean, let's face it, I wasn't going to be much good at guarding a car if I happened also to be holding a baby. Two babies. One on the outside and one on the inside, and the one on the inside was being extraordinarily wiggly. Maybe he or she was jealous.

Or maybe not.

Anyway, I rationalized uneasily, it didn't matter how good I was going to be at guarding a car that

didn't need to be guarded, and this one didn't, because it was empty and Salazar was between the car
and the store as well as between me and the store. So
Fletcher—if this was Fletcher's car—was going to
have to go past Salazar to get to the car or, for that
matter, to me, and Salazar wasn't going to let that
happen, except for one thing.

The car wasn't empty.

Its driver was crouching over so that nobody could
see him, and as soon as Salazar walked around the
corner going toward the door of the Seven-11 the
driver straightened up and the car started and peeled
out, and as the car went by I saw a girl try to sit up.
Lorie. Lorie, and Fletcher backhanded her and she
went back down again.

"Salazar!" I yelled, but Salazar had seen it go,
and he was back in the car beside me almost before I
finished shouting.

I have never before been in a high-speed chase
while holding a baby. I most devoutly hope that I am
never again in a high-speed chase holding a baby. Of
course my seat belt was buckled, but even so, if we
crashed, that baby was going to be crushed between
me and the front of the car. Police cars do not come
equipped with those nice safe baby carriers.

Yelling at Salazar to be careful would have been
futile. He had undoubtedly already decided exactly

how careful he was and was not going to be. He was driving with one hand, yelling into the radio for backups, but where were the backups supposed to come from? He'd already told me he had only two cars on the street, and one of them now was guarding the crime scene.

Then I realized he was on state radio; he was calling for San Miguel County deputy sheriffs. I had no idea of how many of them there might be, or how long it might take them to get into position.

"What he wants," Salazar shouted to me over the sound of the siren, "is to lose us and then get back to that house. He thinks the baby is still there."

"How do you know?" I yelled back. "He's awfully stupid if he thinks we'd go off and leave a baby with a corpse, and I don't think he's that stupid."

"Then I don't know what he wants, except to get away."

Which, unfortunately, he was doing. A Camaro is not made to outrun police, but on the other hand this was by no means a wealthy town, and it could not afford the souped-up patrol cars large cities usually have. The Camaro had a better engine than the Salazar's Ford, and, once again, the Camaro was getting away.

"I'm losing him," Salazar yelled into the radio. "He's going south on Seventh, he's passed Mills, I think he's headed for the Interstate."

If he managed to reach Interstate 85, he could head south for Albuquerque or north for Denver with a minimum of difficulty, and there were plenty of side cutoffs where he could hide just about as long as he wanted to. Hide himself, and hide Lorie. Temporarily or forever.

"Ten-four, Salazar, we've got a roadblock at Mills and Baca."

"Garza, that you?"

"Affirmative."

"He's going hell for leather."

"He won't get past us. We've got a three-car roadblock."

Salazar slammed the brakes. "That's the sheriff," he told me. "Things may get hairy now. I want you to get out. I'm not going to take a baby into a possible shootout. I'll have somebody pick you up."

"Salazar, Lorie's in that car," I yelled. "At the road-block—they need to know—"

"What?"

"Lorie is in the Camaro! I saw her—"

"I'll tell them. Don't worry, we won't let her get hurt."

And then he was gone, still heading south on what was, presumably, Seventh. Whether it was Seventh Street, Seventh Avenue, or Seventh Road I hadn't the slightest idea and cared less. All I cared about was that I was standing on the side of the road holding a baby and needing to go to the bathroom, which was perfectly ridiculous. I ignored the urge and presently it went away, leaving me with a miserable backache.

In less than a minute I was in a second Las Vegas police car, this one driven by a patrol officer named Julia Vasquez. "I've got orders to get you right to the police station," she told me. "It's just about five blocks—"

In those five blocks, we heard a lot of yelling over the radio. Whether or not the Camaro *could* get past those three San Miguel County sheriff's cars, the fact was that the Camaro *did* get past those three San Miguel County sheriff's cars, and nobody was able to fire at him because there was a girl in the car. A kidnap victim, a hostage.

As Salazar had promised, they were trying to protect Lorie, but if Fletcher got away with her...

One deputy was badly hurt and they were yelling for an ambulance, and two other deputies were trying to get the one car that remained drivable out of the pileup to go after the Camaro, which of course was completely out of sight by now. Salazar hadn't been close enough to be in the wreck, but he had lost even more time getting around the wreckage even though he hadn't stopped. Now nobody knew where the Camaro had gone. He'd headed west on Baca, which meant nothing to me but obviously meant a lot to Vasquez, and she glanced quickly at me with that look on her face that indicated she was wondering whether to obey orders and take me to the police station, or whether to take off west on Baca herself.

There were sheriff's cars at Mills and 85, and 104 and 85—I knew that because both announced their locations—and neither of them had seen him. They kept on not seeing him.

That, Vasquez told me, meant that he wasn't on 85. Because if he was on 85 he would have to go by one or the other of those cars, unless he had gotten onto 85 and decided to stop there and sit in the middle of the road, which didn't seem a bit likely.

Obviously Salazar's suggestion that Fletcher thought the baby was still at the house was too silly for words and he wouldn't have come up with it if he'd had time to think. Fletcher couldn't possibly think that, but if he was smart enough to realize the first thing we would do with the baby was to take it to the police station, then he might be doubling back to the police station himself. Because if Ione had been telling the truth, even if Fletcher didn't care about anybody else, he cared about this baby. He wanted this baby. Probably he'd left the baby in the house to start with because he thought he'd get away with it, and then he'd get the baby automatically because he was the father. But that was before he'd killed April, that was before he'd kidnapped Lorie. Now to get the baby he'd have to take it any way he could.

I suggested that to Vasquez and she said, "Oh, shit, then we better get you inside—"

She picked up speed. "If he's headed for the PD then most likely he's doubling back on National," she told me.

The police station is at National and Fourth. Even I knew that.

Vasquez pulled up across the street from the police station and then she thought better of that and made a U-turn, to let me out as close to the door as she could without driving up in the yard where the way was rather obstructed with flagpoles and high curbs and things like that. I got out of the car.

And then I saw the Camaro across the street, the Camaro edging toward me but beginning to pick up speed.

What did I do then?

What do you think I did?

Backache or no backache, I ran like hell, that's
what I did.

TEN

As I DASHED INTO the lobby of the police station, the dispatcher was already buzzing for Salazar's door to unlock itself; Vasquez must have radioed her what was going on. I opened the door and set Scotty Fletcher inside Salazar's office on the floor, where he was safe, where he could not roll off of anything, and where nobody could get to him until and unless the dispatcher pushed the button to open the door again.

Then, with Salazar's door closed securely behind me and my pistol in my hand, I turned to go back out the door to see what I could do about getting Lorie out of that red Camaro.

I did not need to do anything. Lorie was out of the red Camaro and coming in the door of the police station.

Coming in the door with her backpack on one shoulder, with a very nice looking, clean looking, preppy looking young man beside her, with one arm around her throat and a very large hunting knife held to her abdomen.

"Where is he?" he yelled at me.

"Where is who?" I demanded.

"Put the gun away or the girl—"

I hastily put the gun away, not back into the shoulder holster, which might have unduly alarmed him, but on the seat of a chair behind me. Obviously I could not possibly turn a baby over to this man, but other than that there was no need whatever to get him any more agitated than he already was.

The dispatcher was on the radio; she was calling all units into the station, and she was trying to raise Begay. By name, not by number, which was how I knew it was Begay she was talking to.

"Shut up!" Fletcher shouted.

"I wasn't saying anything," I said meekly.

"Tell her to shut up!" He nodded his head toward the dispatch office.

I looked at the dispatcher. "He wants you to shut up."

She was silent. But she'd gotten it out on the air; there wasn't anything else she had to say now and she and I knew it even if Darren Fletcher didn't.

The door opened behind Fletcher, and he half turned, not enough for me to do anything about him—he turned and backed up against the wall so that he could see everybody in the small anteroom and nobody could get behind him.

Salazar was standing in the doorway, with his pistol in his hand. "Drop it!" Fletcher yelled.

"Now, I don't think I want to do that," Salazar drawled.

"I said—"

"Let's think this through," Salazar said, in a very calm voice. "You've got one bargaining chip right now, and that's the girl. That means if you do anything to hurt her you don't have any chips left. So you can't do anything to her. Now, I can't shoot you because you've got the knife on the girl. So right now we've got what is called a Mexican standoff. You can't do anything and I can't do anything. But if I put down the gun then you've got the balance of power. So I'm not going to do that."

"But if I turn loose of the girl then you've got the balance of power," Fletcher retorted.

"Precisely. And that's why it's called a standoff. I don't know why a Mexican standoff, that's just—"

"So I want to bargain."

"Right," Salazar said. "Let's bargain. That way nobody gets hurt."

"Where's the baby?"

"Now, I just don't know where that baby is," Salazar said.

"Don't give me that shit! I saw that lady bringing him in here, and now—"

"*I* didn't see—"

"I didn't say you saw—"

Keep them talking, that is the very first rule of negotiating a hostage situation. Keep them talking, keep negotiations going on, but don't give away anything that matters. That is easy enough to do when you've got a room or an airplane full of hostages and several kidnappers who want to negotiate and have to confer among themselves at every step. But I couldn't imagine how Salazar was going to keep it going for long in this situation, when there was one known killer holding one girl at knifepoint and wanting only one thing.

I suspected Salazar was wondering about that too; I could see—and hoped Fletcher could not see—signs of severe strain around his eyes.

"Somebody better tell me where that baby is—" He pushed the knifepoint against the blue denim covering Lorie's stomach, not enough to hurt her but more than enough to scare her, and she squealed.

"The baby is not in here," I said. "Surely you can see that."

"I saw—"

"I can't help what you saw, the baby is not in here."

"Then where the hell is he?"

"He is in a very safe place," I said. "Mr. Fletcher—"

"How'd you know my name?"

"Do you think we're stupid?" Salazar said contemptuously. "We've known your name for days and days. You left a trail a mile wide."

"You're lying—"

"All right, then how do *you* think we knew your name?"

Fletcher gulped.

I needed to go to the bathroom. Desperately, so desperately I was afraid for a moment I was going to have an accident that even in this situation would be embarrassing. But again the urge went away, leaving me as before with a severe backache. I saw Salazar glance at me and then at his watch, which under the circumstances seemed a very odd thing to do.

"Why'd you do it, Fletcher?" Salazar asked. "I mean, you don't have any kind of past record, at least nothing major. You're no killer. So what made you suddenly decide to—"

"She lied to me!"

"She? Which one? Jill or April?"

"They both lied to me. Everybody always lies to me—I'm sick of being lied to—now that fat lady is lying to me—"

"I am *not* fat," I said. "I'm pregnant. And I'm not lying."

"You said my baby isn't here and I saw you come in the door with him, so don't give me that—"

"I didn't say your baby is not here. I said he is not *in* here, and I said your baby is in a safe place, and he is. Why'd you go off and leave him like that for days and days anyway? I wouldn't—"

"You were s'posed to find him—"

"*I* was supposed to find him? Really, Fletcher! I don't even live in this state!"

"*Somebody* was s'posed to—"

"So you were just going to let him lie there and starve to death and die of thirst in that hellhole of a house because you expected somebody else to take care of him! What kind of a father are you, anyway?"

"You can't say that to me! Listen, I love my baby—"

"Then you have a piss-poor way of showing it!"

"Well, what about *you*? You don't have to do anything so hard—all you have to do is give me my son in exchange for your daughter, and then I'll leave."

"She's not *my* daughter," I said, in as indifferent a tone as I could manage.

I'd have to explain to Lorie, later, how it works, this negotiating to try to keep anybody from getting hurt. Or, no, I wouldn't either, because she was a cop's daughter too, and her mother must have told her about this sort of thing, because she winked at me. I could see it. Fletcher, of course, could not.

"Look, I'm not asking much," Fletcher said. "I just want my kid. My kid, and a half hour head start."

"So you're already adding to what you want?" Salazar said. "Last time you just wanted your kid. Now you want your kid and a half hour head start. What are you gonna want next time, your kid and a half hour head start and the Taj Mahal?"

Whenever you are in a crisis situation, the surest thing of all is that the unexpected is bound to happen. This shouldn't even have been unexpected.

The baby started to cry.

The door to the chief's office wasn't completely soundproof, and although faint, the wailing was quite audible. Fletcher's head turned sharply in that direction, and Salazar took two steps toward Fletcher, preparing to rush him, but Fletcher must have had a wide peripheral vision. He caught the movement, and his head whisked back toward Salazar. "Don't try it," he said, jerking on Lorie's head as a reminder.

I decided to talk to Lorie instead of to him. "Lorie, are you okay?"

"Yeah," she said, "I guess. Only I want to go home."

"We'll get you home."

"Only if you do exactly as I say," Fletcher said.

"Okay, you want the baby and a half hour head start and the Taj Mahal and what else?" Salazar demanded.

"All I asked for is my baby and a half hour head start."

Salazar shrugged. "Then get your baby. If you can."

He glanced at the dispatcher and shook his head very slightly.

Fletcher backed around so that he was standing by the door to Salazar's office. Then it dawned on him that he could not simultaneously keep one hand around Lorie's neck, keep a knife at Lorie's throat, and turn a door knob. "Open the door," he ordered Lorie.

Lorie reached for the door knob. "I can't. It's locked."

"I said *open the door!*"

"I can't open the door, you stupid idiot," Lorie screamed. "Can't you get it through your head that the *stupid door is locked!*"

Fletcher turned to Salazar. "What room is that anyway?"

"It's my private office."

"Open the door."

"I can't. It's locked."

"Your own private office and you can't open the door? Come on, man, open the door!"

"The girl told you, it's locked."

"Then unlock it! You said it's your office, you unlock the door!"

"I'll have to find the keys. Just a minute." With his left hand—his right hand was still holding his pistol, and as heavy as the pistol looked, his arm must be getting some more kind of tired—Salazar got the keys to his patrol car out of his pocket. "Car keys," he said. He dropped them onto a chair. He got out his wallet. "Wallet." He dropped it onto a chair. He dropped a handful of change out onto the chair. "Coins." He turned his pockets inside out. "That's all. No keys. Sorry. I must've left them on my desk."

"Then how'd she get the baby in there?"

"I must've left the door open awhile ago and now it's shut." Salazar smiled blandly at Fletcher.

"Then how are you gonna get back in there?"

"Maybe I'll have to call a locksmith."

Fletcher nodded toward the dispatcher. "Can she get in there? Is there another door?"

"There's another door but she can't get in there. It's locked from the inside too."

"You could shoot the lock off the door."

"I could," Salazar agreed. "Deb, where is the baby?"

"I put him just inside the door. But of course you know they crawl around so much at that age."

"He's six months old," Fletcher objected. "Babies that age don't crawl."

Salazar and I both laughed, almost genuinely, at that. "Mister, I got six kids," Salazar said. "I guarantee you, they sure as hell crawl. Or if you don't want to say crawl they scoot on their stomachs. Every one of mine, before they got home from the hospital, the nurses kept having to pull them down to the foot of the bassinet and two minutes later they'd be banging their heads against the top of the bassinet and howling because there was something in the way and they couldn't go any farther. Mister, there's a lot of metal in that room. If a bullet gets in that room it's going to ricochet and it might go anywhere. That's your baby, but it's my gun, and if you think I'm going to take a chance on shooting a baby you can go straight to hell. Which is your ultimate destination anyway at the rate you're going, but—"

"Then how'm I gonna get my baby?"

"I'd say you've got a problem."

"People always lie to me."

"Then you listen to me, Fletcher," Salazar said, "because I'm going to tell you the exact truth. Every word I'm telling you now is true. That door is locked, I do not have a key to that door. And if I did have the key—which you know I don't because you saw me empty my pockets—I'd do anything in the world to keep you from getting that baby. Sure, I'd lie to you. I'm not lying now, but I would lie to you, and I would kill you if I had to, though I've never killed anybody yet and I'm not too eager to start now. There's no way I'm going to let you get your hands on that baby."

"He's my baby!"

"What makes him your baby?"

"I'm his father."

"So what? So you screwed Jill Montrose and got her pregnant and then married her because you were so proud of your virility. Big man Darren Fletcher, he's got a dick and it works. So what, so does half the human race. So does a billy goat. Does that make you fit to be a father? Prove to me you could take decent care of that baby—prove to me you *would* take decent care of that baby—and I'll find a way to get that door open and let you have him. But you've got to prove it first.''

"You know why I killed Jill? She was gonna give my baby away, that's why. What would you do if your wife was gonna give your kids away?''

"My wife and I take care of each other. How did you take care of Jill? You walked out on her. You walked out on her and left her pregnant. What the hell kind of a man do you call yourself anyway?''

"Yeah but—''

"Yeah but what? You walked out on Jill and left her to have the baby by herself. Where were you when that baby was born? Where were you when Jill was getting up at two o'clock in the morning to feed him?''

"You don't understand!'' Fletcher yelled. "She wasn't nice to me!''

"And you're so nice yourself, standing there with a knife stuck in a girl's side. What did she ever do to you?''

"She—she's just like April.''

"How's she just like April?''

"April lied to me! She said she was gonna have a baby and then she—I found out—''

"You found out what? That April decided a baby would be better off never getting born than getting born to a father like you? To a father who'd do what you did to Jill? Did you tell April about that?''

''I told her—''

''What did you tell her? Did you take her to see Jill, after—''

''I wouldn't—''

''I don't believe you. There's nothing you wouldn't do. What are you doing right now? That girl is fifteen years old. Why are you hurting her?''

''She was with April—she and April were at that place—''

''Monday morning? April got her abortion Monday morning. You took her there. Monday morning that girl you're tormenting right now was hitchhiking from Santa Fe to Los Alamos with her boyfriend.''

''She met April at that place—''

Then, suddenly, Lorie realized what she was being accused of. ''You're saying *I* got an abortion? Deb, is that what he's saying? You son-of-a-bitch, I never was pregnant, I never did anything to *get* pregnant—you *bastard*—don't you *dare* talk about me that way!'' She started kicking, stopping only when Fletcher jabbed the point of the knife hard enough to break at least the top layer of denim if not her skin.

"Yeah," Salazar shouted, "that's really the way to show me you're fit to be trusted with a baby, isn't it, hurting a girl? That really makes a hell of a lot of sense."

We—Salazar and I, and partly Lorie, but mostly Salazar—were doing a real good job of engaging Fletcher in conversation. But it wasn't accomplishing one damn thing. We still had a Mexican standoff; Fletcher still had Lorie and there still wasn't anything either Salazar or I could do to get Lorie away from him unharmed.

By now I was quite certain that the building was surrounded, that the rest of the city employees had been quietly evacuated from the adjoining city offices. This building now contained only the dispatcher, Salazar, the baby, Lorie, Fletcher, and me. There were probably city police cars, what few were on duty, and county sheriff's cars, as many as were available, and probably a few spare troopers or highway patrol or whatever they call themselves in New Mexico gathered around outside.

But none of that did any good to us inside.

We still had to figure out what to do about the present situation, and there wasn't much of anything to do about it, not and keep Lorie unharmed. Salazar couldn't shoot; even if he shot to kill and his aim was perfect Lorie would almost certainly be badly hurt, even if it was no more than a dying reflex muscle action that tightened that arm around her throat or drove that long-bladed knife into her body.

So one of us—almost certainly Salazar—was going to have to rush Fletcher. And again, the chances were that Lorie was going to get hurt when that happened. Salazar, like me, like just about any other police officer, was willing—if somewhat less than eager—to take chances for himself, but somewhat unwilling to take them for anybody else. The only problem was that there didn't seem to be anything else to do.

For a moment everybody had run out of words. It was a *tableau vivant*, Fletcher with the stranglehold on Lorie, Salazar with his pistol at arm's length (and he was going to be physically incapable of holding that pose much longer—if you don't believe it, try holding a heavy book at arm's length for ten minutes), me standing in the middle of the room.

I still needed to pee. Salazar had said *Hal* needed a bladder transplant, but it was becoming more and more evident that *I* needed a bladder transplant.

The baby was still crying faintly. I didn't guess it would hurt him; he couldn't be hungry again (well, he could, considering how long he'd gone unfed before I fed him an hour ago, but it wouldn't harm him to wait a little longer).

Then there was a commotion out in the street. Several males were shouting at one another, and one voice I could make out was definitely that of Hal. What, I wondered apprehensively, was he up to? With everything else, the last thing I needed was Hal in here.

Somebody outside agreed with me. Somebody was yelling, "Keep out of there," and there was more commotion; it sounded as if somebody was wrestling on the front steps. Then the front door burst open and Hal and Begay were inside.

They both stopped short, taking in the scene. Hal had glanced at me briefly, just enough to register my presence, before his eyes settled on Fletcher and Lorie.

What happened next was something an adult would never have tried. Salazar or I or even Begay—we would have known it wouldn't work, and so we wouldn't have tried it. Or we would have known that even if it did work the chances of Lorie getting hurt would be too great, and so we wouldn't have tried it.

But Hal is bigger than Salazar, and bigger than Begay, and bigger than me. He's taller, and he's got more reach, and he's got longer legs.

And the mental connections in his mind between cause and effect are not nearly so great as one could reasonably hope.

Which means that he didn't know it was impossible, and he didn't know that it was too dangerous to risk.

Oh yes, and Hal plays soccer. A lot of soccer.

His face didn't announce what he was going to do, as my face or Salazar's face undoubtedly would have done.

He simply kicked.

With the full length of his long legs and with all the force he could muster, he kicked high and accurately, and the knife went into the air and I started to scramble for it and then thought better of that idea and just got out of the way fast to let it fall.

With the knife gone, Lorie was no longer immobilized. She twisted around in the grasp Fletcher still had—though not nearly so tightly—around her neck, and raised her knee viciously, planting it directly in his groin.

All that left for Salazar to do was grab Fletcher who was trying to double up and clutch his groin, swing him around and shove him hard against the wall, and handcuff him. The siege was over. Salazar told the dispatcher to notify everybody outside that everything was covered and they could go back on patrol.

As a couple of sheriff's deputies apparently bent on being sure nobody was being forced to send out false radio messages came in, the dispatcher buzzed the office door and I opened it. That started Fletcher yelling again about lies and lying.

"Nobody lied to you," Salazar told him.

"You need help, Salazar?" somebody in a brown uniform asked, and somebody else in a brown uniform said, "You okay, Chief?"

"Everything's under control," Salazar said. "No, we don't need anything now. Thanks for the backup. It could have got real hairy."

"That was what it sounded like. Well, if you're sure . . ."

"I'm sure." He turned to Fletcher, as I picked up the baby, whose only complaint at present seemed to be the condition of his diaper and the hardness of the floor. "I didn't lie to you," Salazar repeated. "I just didn't tell all of the truth."

"Yeah, you said you'd give me my baby."

"If you could convince me you could and would take care of him, right. Well, guess what, Fletcher, you didn't convince me. Now you listen for a minute. You have the right to remain silent . . ."

Leaving Salazar giving a Miranda warning, I handed the baby to Lorie and took off to the rest room. I noticed just as I left that Salazar paused in his recital to glance quickly at his watch, but I didn't think anything of that. It was perfectly normal to want to know what time it was. This had been an extremely chaotic day so far and it showed few signs of improving, at least in terms of chaos, though in terms of crisis it had abruptly become a whole lot better.

When I got back from the rest room, the baby was gone and Fletcher was sobbing with his head on the desk. "What happened?" I asked sharply.

"Nothing happened," Salazar said. "Welfare just picked up the baby." I felt momentarily sad; I would have liked to see him again before . . . But then I realized it was better this way. If I had seen him many more times I would have wanted to keep him, and obviously I couldn't. But maybe he'd be lucky. Maybe his grandmother would decide she was too old to raise a baby, and he could go to that nice lady in San Francisco, the one who had worried about him without ever having seen him.

Fletcher raised his head. "You don't understand," he said. "You don't understand. I'm not a killer."

"No?" Salazar said. "You sure could have fooled me.'

"*You* said I'm not a killer."

"So I changed my mind."

"You don't understand."

"You want to try to explain? You don't have to—"

"I'm not stupid," Fletcher said. "I know what I signed. I know I don't have to tell you anything. But I want you to understand. I'm not a killer. Not really. I— it was—Jill was going to give the baby away."

"Why?"

"She said she was scared I would hurt him, but I wouldn't—"

"Why was Jill scared you would hurt the baby?"

"Well—"

"Well, why? You want to tell me or not?"

"You don't understand."

"You ain't shitting."

"What?"

"You're right," Salazar said, "I don't understand. But I'll be glad to listen to an explanation. Why was Jill afraid you'd hurt the baby? Did you hurt Jill?"

"Well, I—"

"We got a lot of calls to your house when you and Jill were living together, remember that?"

"Yeah but, she wouldn't do what I told her to."

"She wouldn't do what you told her to. Like what?"

"Anything. Stuff I told her to do and she wouldn't do it."

"Give me an example."

Lorie, Hal, and Begay were watching from the door to the chief's office; Fletcher's back was to them, and I wasn't sure he even remembered they were there. Fletcher was handcuffed and subdued, and Salazar was gradually sliding down in his chair the same way he had done when he was talking to Hal; his attitude seemed to invite confidences.

"Well—just anything. Like I'd tell her I wanted dinner at six-thirty and then it wouldn't be ready."

"Why?"

"I don't know why, it ought to be—"

"What kind of reason did she give?"

"Oh, like she didn't get home in time and the dishes weren't washed—I don't see why she couldn't wash the dishes while she was cooking supper, or in the morning before she left for school—my mother always—"

"Let's see, you walked out in September and the baby was born in October. That means Jill was seven months pregnant. She was seven months pregnant and going to school. What else was she doing?''

''Oh, she had this part-time job, but it wasn't much. She was just working in an office.''

''You ever work in an office?''

''No, but—''

''Then how do you know it wasn't much? What time did she get home?''

''Five-fifteen, and that's plenty of time to wash dishes and make supper before—''

''And you were in school full time, right?''

''Yeah.''

''So what time did you get home?''

''Three-thirty. What does that have to do with—''

''You know how to wash dishes?''

''It wasn't my job!''

''Washing dishes was Jill's job. Cooking supper was Jill's job. What was your job?''

''Well, I—I'm a handworker.''

''I see. What was your job at home?''

''I made stuff.''

''You made stuff. Gloryosky. So Jill didn't have dinner ready so you slammed her around until the neighbors heard the commotion and called the cops, and then you finally left her. Why'd you leave her?''

''Why should I stay with her? She wouldn't do what I told her. My mom always—''

"Always did what your dad told her? Well, then maybe your dad did stuff for her in return. Do you think so?"

"It wasn't my job—"

"You make me sick," Salazar said, sitting up quite rapidly. "You love babies? You love kids? Let me tell you something, punk. You don't know what a baby is. You're just like some little girl in the slums who gets pregnant accidentally on purpose and tells the social worker it's so she'll have somebody who'll love her because nobody else does. What do you think a baby is? Do you think it's like a kitten or a puppy? Even a kitten or a puppy has needs. Do you think a baby is like a doll or a stuffed toy, that you play with when you want to and neglect the rest of the time? That's not the way it is. Babies yell. They cry. Sometimes they cry all night. They have to get fed—every three or four hours, to start with. They make messes. They shit in their diapers and have to get changed. They learn to walk by themselves but you have to teach them to talk. They take a lot of time. Self-centered me-firsters don't need babies. They don't know how to take care of babies. What would you have done with that baby? You'd have got tired of him in a week and gone off and left him in somebody's garbage can."

Involuntarily I shivered. I knew a baby that had happened to. Fortunately she had been rescued in time.

"Now, you can call me a heathen if you want to," Salazar went on. "Because I don't have any kind of religion you probably ever heard of. I have my mother's religion. But my daddy was Catholic and I was raised Catholic until I changed my mind when I was grown up. Well, one thing I didn't change my mind on was abortion. I don't like abortion. I don't think it's right. But I'll tell you something, if April had to choose between aborting that baby she was carrying, and letting you get your sorry hands on it, then I'd say she made the right decision. And you call yourself a man. Shit. You make me sick."

"You don't—"

"Understand. Right. I don't understand. That's only page one. I don't want to understand. I don't want to be the kind of man that could understand you. Begay, lock him up."

I was glad he was going to be locked up, because if he had kept on talking I would have felt constrained to keep on listening, and I needed—well, you can guess what I needed.

And once again Salazar glanced at his watch as I left, trailing shreds of dignity.

When I returned, Salazar was talking quietly with Lorie, who was a lot calmer than I expect I would have been if I had gotten into the same situation when I was fifteen.

"We went back up to that park," she was saying, "because he liked camping up there. He wanted me to... to... to *do it* with him in that kiva thing because he said it was magic and I told him I wouldn't. He said he wouldn't rape me and he didn't but he was mad..."

"So that's how the scarf got in there?" I asked.

"Yeah." She glanced at me. "I'm sorry, I didn't mean to lose your scarf."

"That scarf is of absolutely no importance, especially compared to getting you back," I assured her. "Anyway, we found it. Lorie, how did he get you to start with?"

"I don't know," she said. "I mean I went to sleep with Hal, I mean not *with* Hal, you know what I mean, by Hal, and then I woke up and I was in the backseat of his car and I was real thirsty and I had this horrible headache—I mean I felt crummy."

"Begay found this in Fletcher's pants pocket," Salazar said, and handed me a bottle of chloral hydrate. Combined with alcohol, chloral hydrate makes a very strong and sometimes lethal knock-out potion often referred to as a Mickey Finn, but even by itself chloral hydrate is a very potent sleeping medication. Dropped into a couple of glasses of iced tea, it could certainly ensure very sound sleep for a couple of tired teenagers.

"And then he kept telling me I was going to take care of his baby, and I tried to tell him I don't know how to take care of a baby, I'm not old enough, but he didn't care. He said I had to because it was my job. I mean he is squirrely. He is some more kind of squirrely."

She went on talking, almost compulsively, and I noticed Salazar had a tape recorder running on his desk. Hal and Begay came back in, and I looked up to see Hal walk over behind Lorie and begin to rub her shoulders, just the way Harry rubs my shoulders when I've been having a really bad day. Well, I thought. Well. Maybe Hal will grow up one of these days after all.

"Begay," Salazar said, "is it okay if Hal spends a few days with you? I don't think we need to keep him locked up anymore, but I don't think he'll be going home quite yet. Lorie, have you had chicken pox?"

"Yes, sir, why?"

"You'll be visiting me for a few days."

"Salazar," I asked, "why aren't they going home yet? There won't be any trouble getting them back for the trial, but you don't really have to have them for the committal hearing, do you? I mean, I know Hal has a court date, but—"

"Oh, I think we'll forget about that," Salazar said blandly. "We can't charge the hero of the hour, can we? Of course if he ever gets into any more trouble and I find out about it—"

"I won't," Hal promised fervently.

"Then why—?"

"Deb," Salazar said, "you've been going—or trying to go—to the bathroom every five minutes for the past two and a half hours. Doesn't that suggest something to you?"

"I have a small bladder, especially right now."

"Oh shit," Salazar said. "I mean *exactly* every five minutes."

I stopped and thought about it. Now that he mentioned it, I did have an awful backache, and I was needing to go to the bathroom again right now. I placed one hand on my abdomen, experimentally.

Yes, that was what I was doing, all right.

I CALLED HARRY as soon as I got to the hospital, to tell him what was going on and be sure he called Lorie's mom. And then I had to go, because I really was kind of busy.

I called Harry again in the middle of the night. We had tentatively agreed on a couple of names, and I wanted to let him know which one we were using.

The next couple of days I got to spend resting and playing with the baby, which was super. Maria Salazar, despite having three children with chicken pox, managed to cope quite adequately with caring for Lorie and bringing me cookies and milkshakes in the hospital. I finally found out why Salazar felt so strongly about adoptions; it turned out half his children were adopted. They'd been children nobody else wanted. I thought they were beautiful, myself. And finally, more than a week after they'd taken off, I got Hal and Lorie back home. Despite all that had happened, they had missed only two days of school.

And I even got to take Harry home from the hospital. He said it was supposed to be the other way around—he was supposed to take me home from the hospital—but I couldn't help that. He's still limping some, but at least he's out of traction.

The only problem now is that I keep thinking I'll be fifty-eight when Cameron—that's my baby's name—is sixteen. Can I cope with these kinds of shenanigans then?

Well, if I can't, he's got an older brother and a couple of older brothers-in-law. I can always send one of them to fetch him home from New Mexico.

Anyway I have taken very good care of myself (now why did Salazar laugh so much when I told him that?) and with any kind of luck at all, Cameron will be healthy despite all the commotion at his birth.

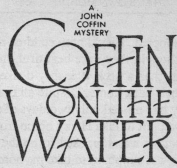

A
JOHN
COFFIN
MYSTERY

COFFIN ON THE WATER

Gwendoline Butler

There was a present coming for legendary actress
Rachel Esthart—at least that's what the note said. A
present from her son.

Odd fact was that her son had been dead for nearly
seventeen years, drowned when he was only five.
Some people still suspected Rachel of murdering
the boy.

"A cleverly plotted, carefully crafted story. Solid fare
for fans of the leisurely British traditional."
—*Kirkus Reviews*

Under the
INFLUENCE

ELIZABETH TRAVIS

A
BEN &
CARRIE
PORTER
MYSTERY

First Time in Paperback

Gorgeous and charming, the talented artist was simply irresistible—even to happily married women like Carrie Porter. But when the egocentric playboy is found shot dead and stabbed in an office at Carrie and Ben Porter's publishing firm, it's clear somebody had had enough of Greg and his mating games.

Ben and Carrie are drawn into the sordid underbelly of raging passions and devious manipulation—and unveil a bloody portrait of a murder.

Can you keep a secret?

You can keep this one plus 2 free novels.